'Where did it come from?' she asked. 'Do you know? The tradition of kissing under the mistletoe, that is.'

Kissing...

Adam stared down at Emma. At the back of her head, where the light was creating those copper glints in her curls. He took a mouthful of his whisky.

'It's very old,' he said. 'I've heard that it got hung somewhere and the young men had the privilege of kissing the girls underneath it, but every time they did they had to pick one of the berries, and when the berries had all been picked the privilege ceased.'

Emma held up the half-finished wreath with its clusters of waxy white berries. 'It's got a lot of them,' she said, tilting her head to smile up at Adam.

That did it. The magic was too strong to resist. Adam put his glass down and then reached out and plucked one of the tiny berries from the wreath.

Emma's eyes widened. 'You can't do that,' she objected. 'You haven't kissed a girl.'

Adam didn't say anything. He just leaned down until there was no mistaking his intention.

And Emma didn't turn her face away. If anything, she tilted her chin so that her lips parted, and for a heartbeat—and then two—she held his gaze.

There was surprise in those blue eyes. She hadn't expected this. But, then, neither had Adam. And she could feel the magic, too—he was sure of that, because there was a kind of wonder in her eyes as well.

Joy was always lurking there, he suspected, but this was an invitation to share it. An invitation no man could resist.

The moment his lips touched Emma's the tiny white berry fell from his fingers and rolled somewhere under the table. Adam wasn't aware of dropping it. He was aware of nothing but the softness of her lips. He cupped desire for more from nowhere

Dear Reader

Many years ago, I lived in Scotland for two years. I loved getting out of Glasgow and into the country villages.

The gorgeous countryside is not unlike my home of New Zealand, but we don't have the magic of the cobbled streets and ancient cottages.

Christmas here is in summer, of course, but I remember the winters in Scotland very well—when the cold and dark days made the lights brighter and the warmth of home so alluring.

What better setting for a Christmas story? Romance has a magic of its own, and so does Christmas. Mixing them together is a recipe for something special. I do hope you enjoy Adam and Emma's story as much as I loved writing it.

Merry Christmas!

With love

Alison xxx

A LITTLE CHRISTMAS MAGIC

BY
ALISON ROBERTS

MILLS & BOON

Published in Great Britain 2014
by Mills & Boon, an imprint of Harlequin (UK) Limited,
Eton House, 18-24 Paradise Road, Richmond, Surrey, TW9 1SR

© 2014 Alison Roberts

ISBN: 978-0-263-90801-5

Alison Roberts lives in Christchurch, New Zealand, and has written over sixty Mills & Boon® Medical Romances™.

As a qualified paramedic, she has personal experience of the drama and emotion to be found in the world of medical professionals, and loves to weave stories with this rich background—especially when they can have a happy ending.

When Alison is not writing, you'll find her indulging her passion for dancing or spending time with her friends (including Molly the dog) and her daughter Becky, who has grown up to become a brilliant artist. She also loves to travel, hates housework, and considers it a triumph when the flowers outnumber the weeds in her garden.

Recent titles by Alison Roberts:

200 HARLEY STREET: THE PROUD ITALIAN◊
FROM VENICE WITH LOVE‡
ALWAYS THE HERO††
NYC ANGELS: AN EXPLOSIVE REUNION~
ST PIRAN'S: THE WEDDING!†
MAYBE THIS CHRISTMAS…?
THE LEGENDARY PLAYBOY SURGEON**
FALLING FOR HER IMPOSSIBLE BOSS**
SYDNEY HARBOUR HOSPITAL: ZOE'S BABY*
THE HONOURABLE MAVERICK

◊*200 Harley Street*
‡*The Christmas Express!*
*Sydney Harbour Hospital
†*St Piran's Hospital*
****Heartbreakers of St Patrick's Hospital*
~*NYC Angels*
††*Earthquake!*

**These books are also available in eBook format
from www.millsandboon.co.uk**

Did you know that THE HONOURABLE MAVERICK won
a 2011 *RT Book Reviews* Reviewers' Choice Award?

It's still available in eBook format
from www.millsandboon.co.uk

Dedication

For Becky—who will always be with me for Christmas,
no matter where she is.
With all my love.

Praise for
Alison Roberts:

'Readers will be moved by this incredibly sweet story
about a family that is created in the
most unexpected way.'
—*RT Book Reviews* on
THE HONOURABLE MAVERICK

'I had never read anything by Alison Roberts
prior to reading TWINS FOR CHRISTMAS,
but after reading this enchanting novella
I shall certainly add her name to my auto-buy list!'
—*Cataromance.com* on
TWINS FOR CHRISTMAS

'Ms Roberts produces her usual entertaining blend of
medicine and romance in just the right proportion,
with a brooding but compelling hero
and both leads with secrets to hide.'
—Mills & Boon® website reader review on
NURSE, NANNY…BRIDE!

CHAPTER ONE

WHAT EMMA SINCLAIR needed right now was a magic wand.

One that she could wave over the calendar on her wall and simply make the month of December vanish.

Turn it into January and the start of a new year. A new life.

Or not.

Maybe she could use the wand not to wish time away but to freeze it. To make it always early December, with her feeling so well she could imagine the last few years had been nothing more than a very bad dream.

It was getting a little stuffy in her tiny London apartment. Emma moved to crack open the window to let some fresh air in for a moment. Very fresh air. The sky was a dark slate and that cloud cover clearly swollen with moisture but it wasn't likely to start falling as pretty snowflakes. A bit of stinging sleet, maybe. Or freezing fog.

London could be so grey at this time of year.

So bleak. It was only mid-afternoon but already there were lights on everywhere. In the street below and in the windows of the apartment buildings she looked out onto. Not just ordinary lights either. Some people already had their Christmas trees up and the row of shops at street level had them in their front windows with multi-coloured lights flashing and twinkling. Somebody was dressed as Father Christmas on the street, too, handing out flyers to passers-by, probably offering a discount on some seasonal service or product.

There were lots of people hurrying about their business, wrapped up in coats and scarfs. Umbrellas were opening as the clouds decided to let go of some of the moisture. Mothers made sure their prams were well covered and tried to juggle parcels and small children to keep them sheltered.

So many people.

Families.

Funny how a crowd could make you feel so much more alone.

The phone ringing was a welcome distraction.

'Sharon… What's the weather like in sunny California?'

'Gorgeous. Doesn't feel right when it's December. And how did that happen? It feels like yesterday that I was having my summer wedding in good ol' Blighty. Is it all grey and freezing?'

'Sure is.' She would need to remember to close the window as soon as she'd finished talking to her closest friend. She stepped closer to the friendly glow of her small, gas fire.

'What are you doing?'

'Right at this minute? I'm looking at one of your wedding photos on my mantelpiece. You were the world's most beautiful bride. You look *so* happy.'

'Aww…I had the best bridesmaid. That helped.'

Emma laughed. 'You were marrying the love of your life—that's what helped. How's Andy?'

'Gorgeous. We were talking about you last night and

he told me to ring. We want you to come and have Christmas with us.'

'Ohhh…' The sound was a mix of frustration and regret. 'I can't. I have to be here for when they call me in. The three-month mark will be late December and they'll have to squeeze me in when they get a space. Jack told me I'd better not go too far away.'

'I feel awful I can't be with you for that. It's such a horrible procedure to have to go through on your own.'

'I'll cope.'

'I want to be with you. To drive you home afterwards and make sure you take your painkillers.'

'I know. It'll be okay, Sharn.'

'You could put it off until the new year…I'm sure that adorable Dr Jack of yours would be happy to oblige.'

Emma had closed her eyes as she took a deep breath. 'The waiting's hard enough without making it longer. I… don't think I could handle that.'

'I understand… It's rotten timing but the sooner it happens, the better. You'll let me know, won't you? The instant you have news?'

'Of course. You'll be the first to know.'

'It'll be good news. I'm totally sure of that.'

'No. It won't be good.' Emma had to swallow hard now. 'It'll either be the best news ever or the worst. No middle ground this time. If it hasn't worked it's the end of the road. Nothing more they can do. Just a matter of time…'

Her words went all wobbly and Emma kicked herself mentally for giving in to voicing her deepest fear. Maybe the uncharacteristic weakness had sneaked up on her because her gaze was resting on other photographs on her mantelpiece. The father she'd lost long ago. Her beloved mother who'd died just over a year ago now.

'You need distraction,' Sharon told her. 'Being cooped up all by yourself isn't helping.'

'You're right. I'm thinking of getting a job.'

'Really? Are you feeling that good?'

'I am. And there are plenty of temporary jobs that come up at this time of year. Do you remember the year that I was an elf?'

'One of Santa's helpers.' Sharon was laughing. 'I'm sure I've got a photo of you in that outfit somewhere. I'd better not show it to Andy or he might think he married the wrong girl.'

'Yeah, right…' But Emma was grinning. 'Or I could busk…' She shifted her gaze to a far corner of the room. 'My poor guitar's just gathering dust at the moment.'

'Sounds cold. Being an elf would be more fun.'

'Yeah…' It was getting cold in the apartment now. Definitely time to close the window. To get moving properly, even. 'You know what? I'm going to go down to the corner shop and get some papers. See what's being advertised under the situations vacant.'

'Go, you! Keep me posted.'

'I will.'

'Love you. Miss you heaps.'

'Same.'

When the call ended, all Emma could hear was the soft hiss of her fire and the patter of rain on the window. After the joy of conversation it was an unpleasant quietness.

A very lonely one.

Threatening. If she stayed in here it would pull her back into her pity party so allowing it to continue wasn't an option. Latching the window, Emma shrugged into her warmest coat and wrapped a scarf around her neck. She slung her bag over her shoulder and picked up her umbrella as she let herself out the door. She wouldn't get the papers at the corner store. She'd walk all the way to the high street and get the bonus of a decent bit of exercise on her mission.

'Ouch… That *hurts*, Daddy.'

'Sorry, pet.'

Adam McAllister suppressed a growl of frustration. Fine blonde hair was refusing to co-operate. How could his fingers be so deft when it came to removing a foreign object or stitching up a wound so that it barely left a scar but be seemingly incapable of braiding a small girl's hair?

'How about a wee ponytail instead?'

'No.' The headshake pulled the almost finished braid from his fingers and what had already been accomplished unravelled at the speed of light. 'Jeannie always has plaits and I want to look the *same*.'

'Dad? Where's my shoe?'

'Where you left it, I expect, Ollie.' Adam picked up the hairbrush again and the movement made him notice the face of his watch. 'It'll have to be a ponytail, Poppy, otherwise you're going to be late for school and I'll be in trouble with Mrs Stewart at the clinic. The waiting room will be full of cross people asking where their doctor's got to.'

Poppy burst into tears.

A crashing sound came from the living room, accompanied by a wail from her twin, Oliver. 'It wasn't my fault. It just falled over and now it's *broken*…'

The wind must have caught the front door to make it slam so loudly. 'I'm sorry I'm so late. The roads are so icy and old Jock was blocking the road with his tractor, helping someone whose wheels were in the ditch. I…' She stopped talking, taking in the scene of chaos in the kitchen.

'I take it she's gone, then?'

'Aye…' Gratefully, Adam pushed the hairbrush into his mother's hand. 'I've almost got the bags ready. I'd better go and see what Ollie's broken.'

'Little minx. I can't believe she's run off like that. With no notice.'

'She's nineteen. In love. Getting pregnant probably made the decision a wee bit urgent.'

'What's pregnant?' Poppy had stopped crying and was standing very still while her grandmother rapidly braided her hair.

'It means that you're going to have a baby.'

'Auntie Marion's going to have a baby.'

'Aye…she is. So's Kylie.'

'But Kylie looks after us. She's coming back, isn't she?'

'No. She's going to Australia—where her boyfriend comes from.'

'What's Australia?'

'It's a country a long way away.' Adam had gone as far as the door to see that the standard lamp had fallen in the living room, sweeping a photograph from the corner of the mantelpiece onto the hearth. Nothing life-threatening. He could sort it out later when he had a minute to spare. Stooping, he picked up an abandoned shoe.

'Ollie? Where are you? It's time for school.'

A small, tousled head with wide eyes appeared slowly from behind the sofa.

'Come and see your gran. You need your hair brushed too.'

'It's even further away than Canada.' By some miracle, his mother had found ribbons to tie on the ends of Poppy's plaits. 'Where Aunty Marion lives.'

She looked up as Adam came back with Oliver in tow

but then her gaze shifted to take in the pile of books and
papers on one end of the kitchen table. A milky spoon
from a bowl of cereal was sitting on top of a school book.
Turning her head to look at the dishes piled up on the
kitchen bench, she clicked her tongue.

'I can't do it,' Catherine McAllister said. 'I'm no'
going to take off for Canada and leave you to cope with
this lot alone.'

'You have to. Marion needs you. The bairn's due next
week.'

'She'll understand.'

'This is my sister we're talking about.' Adam's smile
was wry. 'She'd never talk to me again. She'd say I've
had years of your help and she only needs you for a few
weeks. It's not her fault my nanny's run off to Australia.'

Catherine raised her gaze to the old clock on the wall.
'You'd better go, son. Or you'll be getting the evil eye
from Eileen Stewart. She's bad enough when an emergency comes in and puts out all the waiting times. I'll
get these wee lambs off to school.'

'Thanks, Mum.' Adam pushed his arms into the
sleeves of a coat that hadn't made it off the back of a
kitchen chair last night. 'And you're not to even think of
cancelling your trip. I've got ads in papers everywhere
for a temporary nanny. I'll find help for while you're
away at least, and then we can worry about something
more permanent.'

'We'll see about that.' Catherine sounded uncon-
vinced. 'My flight's not till Tuesday. If you haven't found
help by then, I'm staying and that's an end to the matter.'

The train from London to Edinburgh arrived on time.
The connecting train Emma needed to get out into the
middle of a Scottish nowhere was clearly less reliable.

The wicked draught coming into the waiting room was chilling her to the bone and Emma huddled between the backpack full of clothes and her guitar case.

How crazy was this?

But that Dr McAllister had sounded so enthusiastic on the phone yesterday. Said he'd pay for her travel if she could come up for an interview and he was sure she'd be suitable so she might as well bring what she needed for the next few weeks and that way, if she was happy to take the position, she wouldn't need to go all the way back to London again.

And it all sounded so perfect. She already had the image of a pretty, old Scottish village with the stone buildings softened by a layer of fluffy snow and the sound of Christmas carols being sung by rosy-cheeked village children. What better place to spend these few weeks of the unbearable waiting? It wasn't as if she would have the responsibility of caring for a tiny baby or something. Looking after six-year-old twins—how hard could *that* be?

A piercing whistle and then a squeal of brakes announced the arrival of her new train. Emma picked up the straps of her backpack with one hand and the handle of the guitar case with the other. Then she put it down again to fish in her coat pocket. To make sure she had the appointment details for the meeting later this afternoon.

Yes. Four p.m. at the medical centre in the village of Braeburn. Only a short walk from the station, apparently. Across the square at the end of the high street and down the street. She couldn't miss it but if she got as far as the village hall she needed to turn around. She'd be able to meet not only the nice-sounding doctor but the children *and* their grandmother.

Gathering her courage, Emma got herself and her

belongings stowed into an eerily empty train carriage. Braeburn didn't appear to be a very popular destination. With no one to distract her with conversation, there was plenty of time to think about what lay ahead in her immediate future.

That last addition of the grandmother to the interview panel was the one that made her a little uneasy. Her imagination could conjure up a fierce, elderly Scot with no trouble at all. Short and wiry, with a hairnet keeping the corrugated-iron waves of her hair in place and a disapproving glare that would miss nothing remotely unsuitable about an applicant.

She'd be the one to convince.

Emma rested her head back on the faded seat and watched green hills and paddocks and the occasional river drift past. Beautiful country. A long, long way from London and big hospitals and fear of what the new year might bring.

She couldn't go back.

She *had* to get this job. It would be a reprieve from the fear. Time out. A family to spend Christmas with even, and wouldn't that be magic?

A touch to her hair reassured her that the unruly curls were suitably restrained. How good was it that her hair had grown back so enthusiastically after all the chemo? It would have been better to have had the time to buy some new clothes, though. She didn't have a skirt or dress to her name and, having lost so much weight, she was swimming in her jeans and pullover. Hardly the outfit to make much of an impression with but it was personality that mattered, wasn't it?

And this Dr McAllister sounded perfectly nice, with his deep voice and broad Scottish accent. A bit brusque maybe. Possibly a little terse after she'd replayed the conversation in her head a few times but he'd definitely sounded keen.

Almost…desperate?

Maybe the children were little monsters that ate nannies for breakfast and the granny would be glaring at her from a corner and constantly criticising her every move. And the doctor would take one look at her and ask what on earth she was thinking—that she could look after his precious children when it was obvious how sick she was herself?

No. Emma slammed a mental door shut on her unfortunately vivid imagination.

Fate was bringing her here. It had been the first advertisement she'd seen and, when she'd rung, the phone had been answered virtually on the first ring. She hadn't even had to queue for a train ticket. It felt like it was meant to happen.

She needed a bit of faith, that was all. Hardly surprising that that particular mental resource was somewhat depleted at the moment but it felt good to scrape a bit up and hang onto it.

Very good indeed.

It felt remarkably like hope.

The village was every bit as pretty as she had imagined with stone buildings and cobbled streets. Not that Emma had time to admire more than a passing impression because the train had been a bit late and now she had to hurry. That it was much darker for the time of day and probably a lot colder than London didn't seem to matter when the brightly lit shop windows revealed colourful decorations already in place.

She found herself smiling when she hurried past a pub called simply The Inn, which had sprigs of holly on the door framing a handwritten sign that said, 'There's plenty of room.' Maybe the innkeeper with the sense of humour was one of the group of people under the streetlamps, installing a massive Christmas tree in the village square that needed men with ropes and a lot of shouting in a brogue so thick it sounded like a foreign language.

Her heart sank, however, when she entered the medical centre and the grandmother of her imagination fixed her with a look that could probably strip paint.

'D'ye have an appointment? The doctor's no' got time for extras unless it's an emergency. Clinic hours are over.'

The bell on the door behind Emma clanged again before the grandmother had finished speaking and her attempt to decipher more than half the words she had just heard was interrupted by a woman's voice.

'I'll take care o' this, Eileen. We're expecting Emma.'

Her jaw dropping, Emma turned to face an elegantly dressed and very beautiful older woman, who was smiling warmly. 'I take it you *are* Emma?'

'Um…yes. And you're…?'

'Catherine McAllister. Adam's mother.' She looked past Emma's shoulder. 'Is Adam in, Eileen?'

'Aye. The wee bairns as well.' The sniff was disapproving. 'I've told the doctor it's no' a good idea, having bairns in there. They'll break something. Or—'

'Why don't you head off early, Eileen?' Catherine was still smiling. 'I know how busy you must be at the moment. Isn't there a choir practice this evening?'

'Aye…well, if you're sure, Mrs McAllister.'

'I'm just sorry I won't be here to hear all the Christmas carols.'

'It's tomorrow you leave, aye?'

'Mmm. I hope so.' She turned back to Emma. 'Adam's sister is having her first baby. In Canada.'

'Oh…how exciting.' Emma couldn't miss the play of emotion on the older woman's face. 'She'll be so happy to have you there. I…I lost my mum last year and I miss her all the time but *that's* when I'll miss her the most, I think.'

When she had a baby? *If* she ever had a baby would be more truthful. But she'd said too much already, hadn't she? Maybe revealed too much as well, judging by the searching look she was getting. Emma bit her lip but Catherine was smiling. Her eyes were full of sympathy and the touch on Emma's arm was more like a reassuring squeeze.

'Come with me, Emma. We'll go and find that son of mine.'

Could she leave her backpack and guitar in the waiting room? About to step away, Emma caught another glare from Eileen that was punctuated by another eloquent sniff. Hastily, she picked up her luggage and followed Catherine across the waiting room and through another door. She was still trying to readjust her mental image of the children's grandmother and, because she wasn't watching, the guitar was at enough of a sideways angle to catch on the door in front of her so she almost fell into what was obviously a consulting room.

The man, who had one hip perched on the edge of a large wooden desk, jerked his head in her direction. The two children, who were on the floor in the middle of a game that involved a stethoscope and bandages, looked up and froze.

There was an awkward silence and Emma could feel herself blushing furiously as she manoeuvred herself into the room. What had possessed her to bring such an unwieldy extra piece of luggage, anyway? Did she think she might go busking in Braeburn's village square if she didn't land this gig of being a nanny?

What made it so much worse was that the doctor who'd sounded nice but brusque on the phone was just as different from what she'd imagined as the grandmother had been. The fuzzy image of a plump and fatherly country GP had just been bombed. Adam McAllister was tall and fit. More than fit. With his jet-black hair, olive skin and sharply defined angles of his face, he was probably one of the best-looking men Emma had ever seen.

Except that he was scowling. While his mother had surprised her by being so unexpectedly nice, the pendulum had swung in the opposite direction now. Adam McAllister looked uncompromising. Fierce. Angry even?

At *her*?

'I'm sorry I'm late,' she said, the words rushing out. 'The train was…it was…' Oh, help. He was looking at her as if he *knew*. Had he somehow managed to access her medical records or something?

'The train's always late.' Catherine was pulling out a chair. She smiled down at the children. 'What's happened here? Has Poppy broken her leg *again*, Ollie?'

'Aye. I'm fixing her.' But the small boy's attention was diverted now. 'Who are *you*?' he asked Emma. 'And what's *that*?'

'I'm Emma. And this is my guitar case.'

'I want to see.'

'Maybe later.' Adam McAllister's offer did not sound promising. 'Your gran's going to take you to see the tree going up in a minute. And then you're going home for your supper.'

'After some proper introductions,' Catherine said firmly. 'Emma—this is Oliver and this is Poppy. Ollie and Poppy—this is Emma…Sinclair?'

'*Miss* Sinclair,' Adam corrected.

'Emma's fine,' said Emma. 'Hello, Poppy and Ollie. You're twins, aren't you?'

They stared at her. They had brown eyes like their father but their hair was much lighter. Poppy still had golden streaks in her long braids. She also had something clutched in her hand.

'Is that Barbie?'

Poppy nodded. 'She's got a pony,' she offered. 'At home.'

'Lucky Barbie. I love ponies.'

'I've got a pony, too.'

'Jemima's not a *pony*,' Oliver said. 'She's a *donkey*.'

Emma blinked. Catherine laughed. 'Adam probably didn't say much on the phone,' she said, 'but there are a few pets at home. Do you like animals?'

'Yes. I had a job in a pet shop once. We had lots of puppies and kittens and rabbits. Oh, and hamsters and mice and rats, too.'

Poppy's eyes were round. 'I *love* puppies. And kittens.'

'I love *rats*,' Oliver said. 'Can I have a rat, Daddy?'

'We've probably got some out in the barn.'

'I want one for a pet. Inside.'

'No.' The word was almost a sigh. 'You can't have a rat, Ollie.'

'But why *not*?' With a bandage unfurling in his hand to roll across the floor, Oliver scrambled to his feet. 'You said I could tell you what I wanted most for Christmas. And I want a *rat*.'

'They smell bad.' Emma had been the cause of what was becoming a family disagreement. She needed to do something. 'And they've got long tails that are all bald and pink and…icky.'

'*Icky?*' Adam was looking at her as if she was suddenly speaking Swahili.

'Icky,' Poppy repeated. She giggled. 'Icky, icky, icky.'

'*You're* icky,' Oliver told her.

'No. *You* are.'

'Time to go,' Catherine decreed. 'You've met Emma and she's met you. Now it's time for her to talk to Daddy.'

In the flurry of putting on coats and hats and gathering schoolbags, Catherine found time to squeeze Emma's hand.

'I do hope you'll still be here when I get back,' she said softly. 'I'd like the chance to get to know you better.'

She managed to say something to Adam as well, just before she ushered the children out of the room. Emma couldn't hear what she said but, as she sank into the chair as the door closed behind Catherine, he was still scowling at her.

Strength. That was what he needed.

This was his one shot at finding the help he needed so that his mother would not cancel her trip to Canada and this young woman was clearly... He closed his eyes for as long as it took to draw in a new breath. A complete flake?

She looked like a refugee from the sixties or something, carrying a guitar and a backpack. So pale he could almost count the freckles scattered over her nose and she was thin enough to have a waif-like air that probably made her look a lot younger than she was. And what was it with those oversized clothes? It reminded him of when Poppy clopped around the house with her feet in a pair of her grandmother's high-heeled shoes and a dress that was trailing around her ankles.

She was so obviously unsuitable that it was deeply disappointing. He'd have to go through the motions of an interview, though—if only to have ammunition for the argument he'd have to have with his mother later. Her whispered impression had been very succinct.

She's lovely. Give her the job, Adam.

How had this musically inclined waif managed to impress Catherine so much in such a short time?

'So…' He did his best to summon a smile. 'You're fond of animals, then?'

'Mmm.' She was smiling back at him. She had blue eyes, he noted. And brown curls that had a reddish glint where the light caught them. 'I am.'

'And children?'

She nodded enthusiastically. 'I like children, too.'

'Do you have any experience with them?'

'I've taught music classes. And…and I had a job working with children over a Christmas period a while back. I loved it.'

Because she'd never quite grown up herself? How many adults would use a word like 'icky' with such relish?

'But you've never been a nanny?'

'No.'

'Do you have any younger brothers or sisters? Friends who have small children?'

'N-no.' The smile was fading now.

'Do you have a full driver's licence?'

'Yes. I've got a motorbike licence, too.'

The image of this child-woman astride a powerful two-wheeled machine was disconcerting.

'I've even got a heavy-vehicle licence. I had a job driving a bus once.'

Maybe that image was even more of a worry. How had she had the strength to even turn such a large wheel? Or was it the overlarge sleeves on her pullover that made her arms look so frail?

'Can you cook?'

'Well…I did have a job in a restaurant once. I—'

But Adam was shaking his head. 'How old are you, Emma?'

'Twenty-eight.'

Really? Only a few years younger than he was? Hard to believe but the surprise wasn't enough to disturb his train of thought. 'Just how many jobs have you had?'

'I don't know,' Emma admitted. 'Quite a lot. I tend to like part-time or temporary work. That's why this job appealed so much. It's only for a few weeks, isn't it?'

'Aye.' But just because he only needed help on a temporary basis it didn't mean that he wanted to employ someone who was incapable of commitment or even reliability, did it?

Perhaps he should have tried to find something permanent instead of a stop-gap, but who went looking to move and start a new position in the weeks right before Christmas? How many people wanted to move to an isolated Scottish village anyway?

His mother was due to drive to Edinburgh tonight, ready for an early departure tomorrow. If he didn't take a chance on Emma, she would cancel her trip and she'd miss the birth of her new grandchild. She'd be miserable and Adam would feel guilty and the children would pick up on the tension and it could quite likely spoil Christmas for all of them. Not that Adam had found much joy in the season in recent years but the children were his priority now, weren't they?

And Emma had made Poppy giggle with that ridiculous word.

That delicious sound of his daughter's merriment echoed somewhere in the back of his head and it was enough to soften the disappointment that Emma was so unsuitable.

'It *is* only for a few weeks,' he heard himself saying aloud. 'But…ach…' The sound encompassed both defeat and frustration. How bad could it be? He really only needed a babysitter for the hours he had to be at work. 'Fine. The job's yours if you want it, Emma.'

'Oh…' Her eyes widened with surprise. 'Yes. Please. But…don't you have other people to interview?'

'You were the last.' She didn't need to know that she had also been the first, did she? 'I'll lock up here and then we'll head off.' He looked at the unusual luggage on the floor beside Emma's chair. 'Is that all you'll need?'

She nodded.

'And you don't mind being here over the Christmas period? You don't have family who will be missing you?'

'No.' She shook her head this time and dipped her chin so that her gaze was hidden, as if she didn't want him to see how she felt about that.

Maybe it stirred too many memories that were too painful—like it did for him? An emotional cocktail of grief and anger that the season of goodwill and family togetherness only served to exacerbate? The thought gave him an odd moment of feeling potentially connected to this pale stranger in her oversized clothes. Or maybe it was the poignant tilt of her head as she looked down.

He shook off the unwelcome sensation. He had more than enough people to worry about, without adding someone else. Emma's job was to make life easier for him for a little while, not to complicate it any further.

'Right, then.' His movements were brisk as he logged out of his computer and flicked off the desk lamp. 'It's getting late. I suppose I'd better take you home.'

CHAPTER TWO

THE DARKNESS OF a winter's night engulfed the vehicle as it left the outskirts of Braeburn village behind.

Emma eyed the dashboard radio controls longingly. Driving anywhere without music was an alien experience for her but Dr McAllister clearly wasn't going to allow distractions while he was driving. Fair enough. It was raining hard now and the lights were catching a mist of white speckles that suggested it was trying to turn into sleet.

Would conversation also be deemed a distraction? She risked a sideways glance and had to tilt her chin upwards. Even sitting down, Adam McAllister was tall. Well over six feet. Walking beside him into the clinic's car park had made Emma feel very small. He hadn't said anything then either, apart from an offer to carry her bag, which had sounded more like a command than an invitation.

Clearly she hadn't really made a good impression on her new employer but at least he was prepared to give her a chance. Any optimism that she could change his mind was fading now, however, as she took in a profile that was stern enough to suggest an inability to suffer fools gladly.

Imagine running the gauntlet of that snappy little terrier of a receptionist in order to see such an unapproachable GP? You'd have to be really sick, Emma decided. And I'll bet his patients never forget to take their pills.

'What?'

The terse query was enough to make Emma jump. Coupled with the effect of Adam taking his eyes off the road to glare at her for a second, it actually made her heart skip a beat, but the fear that she might have spoken aloud was forgotten as fast as it had appeared.

In the dim reflected light of the dashboard controls, Adam's eyes looked black under equally dark brows. His hair was long enough to be a little unruly and a single lock had detached itself from the rest to flop across his forehead. The crazy desire to reach out and put that curl back where it belonged was so inappropriate that Emma caught her breath in an audible gasp.

She must have sounded as if she'd suddenly decided she might be in the company of an axe murderer, given the way those dark brows lifted. With his gaze safely back on the road, Adam sounded vaguely uncomfortable with the effect he'd had.

'I thought I heard you say something,' he muttered. 'About the hills.'

'Oh…' Emma turned to stare ahead through the windscreen but her gaze caught Adam's hand on the steering-wheel as she did so. He had long fingers and neatly cut nails and…dear Lord…a wedding ring? Why hadn't he mentioned his wife? Why hadn't she been at the interview instead of his mother? Confused, Emma struggled to find a response to his comment. 'It *is* hilly, isn't it? Do you live far from the village?'

'Only another mile or so. Don't worry, you'll have a car to use.'

'Wow…that's great.' Personal transport was an unexpected bonus. 'Thank you.'

The soft snort sounded exasperated. 'You'll need it. There's a lot of driving involved in getting the children to where they need to be. Poppy has a Highland dance class once a week and Oliver is starting drumming lessons in addition to his bagpipes class. On top of that, the school does a nativity play and there'll be rehearsals almost every day after school. You'll also be responsible for grocery shopping and other chores, like going to the vet. One of the dogs is having treatment at the moment for a foot injury.'

Emma was trying to listen carefully to her job description but she was still thinking about the mysteriously absent wife. And then it was too easy to get distracted by the cadence of Adam's deep voice and the gorgeous accent. She only realised she was smiling when she caught the movement of his head as it turned in her direction again. Hastily, she rearranged her face.

'I'm so sorry to hear that. I hope it's nothing serious.'

'A torn pad, that's all. But I didn't notice in time and it got infected.'

Although it looked like they were in the middle of nowhere, Adam put the indicator on and slowed the vehicle, turning through a gap in a tall stone wall. The headlights shone on what looked like a scene from a gothic movie, with the bare branches of massive old trees twisting out to meet each other and create a tunnel—the smaller branches like claws reaching out towards Emma. She shivered.

'It'll be warm inside.'

Startled, Emma looked sideways but Adam was concentrating on driving around the biggest lumps the tree roots were making in the driveway. He couldn't possibly have seen her shiver unless he had exceptionally acute peripheral vision. She hadn't forgotten the way he'd looked at her in his clinic either…as if he knew something she'd rather he didn't know.

A prickle of sensation ran down her spine. She really needed to curb her overactive imagination. Any minute now and she'd have Mrs McAllister buried somewhere down that spooky driveway and she'd be going into the rather forbidding-looking two-storeyed stone farmhouse to find it devoid of a friendly grandmother or any children. There would just be a dark hallway and a ticking grandfather clock and Dr McAllister would shut the door behind her and turn the lock and say—

'So…here we are, then.'

She made an odd squeaking sound as Adam took on his role in her wild train of thought with such perfect timing but then the absurdity of it all surfaced and she had to stop herself laughing aloud.

And then—unexpectedly—she got a rush of pure relief. She'd come here in the hope of finding a distraction from the fear of waiting for news that would have her imagining only her own funeral. Well…she'd already succeeded, hadn't she? She hadn't given her upcoming tests a moment's thought since she'd arrived in Braeburn.

She found herself beaming at her new employer. 'I'm excited,' she confessed. 'I do love starting a new job.'

'So it would seem,' Adam said drily. 'Let's go inside, shall we?'

He led Emma in to the vaulted hallway of the house his family had owned for generations, making a mental note not to forget to wind the grandfather clock this week, heading straight for the door from which the most light was spilling, along with the sound of voices and laughter.

The kitchen. The heart of his home.

Halfway there they were mobbed by the dogs, who

gave their master only a perfunctory welcome before investigating the interesting new arrival. Adam paused to watch the effect, knowing that if Emma had been less than honest about liking animals, it would show up in a matter of seconds. And if she didn't like dogs, she probably didn't like children either and he'd know if he'd made a huge mistake in bringing her into his home.

Almost knocked off her feet by fluffy paws being planted on her stomach, Emma gave a startled exclamation but then her voice was stern.

'Paws on the floor, please,' she commanded. 'And then I can pat you.'

Amazingly, the dogs sat promptly, gazing adoringly up at the newcomer. Emma dropped to her haunches, abandoning her guitar case in favour of cuddling the animals. Getting her face washed enthusiastically, she was laughing as she looked up at Adam.

'They're gorgeous. And so…*hairy*.'

'That's Benji. He's a beardie. And Bob's the Border collie.' Part of him wanted to smile back at Emma but another part was fighting a sense of…disappointment? His new employee had passed this test with flying colours, hadn't she?

It looked like he was stuck with her for the foreseeable future.

The children weren't far behind the dogs.

'Emma—Emma! Gran says you're going to be looking after us now.' With practised ease, Poppy squeezed past the dogs to grab Emma's hand. 'Come with me. I want to show you Barbie's pony. And her caravan. And her swimming pool.'

Oliver eyed the guitar case and then his father. 'It's "later" now, isn't it, Dad?'

'Ach…' Catherine came out of the kitchen door, wiping her hands on her apron. 'Let's give Emma a wee bit o' time to get settled, shall we? Come on. All of you. Supper's almost ready.'

Adam left the backpack he'd been carrying beside the clock. Poppy kept hold of Emma's hand to show her where to go, with Benji following as closely as possible. Oliver picked up the guitar case, which was as big as he was, and struggled in their wake. Bob stayed sitting and held up a bandaged paw.

'I know.' Adam stooped to scratch the hopefully pricked ears. 'I need to take care of that paw but it'll have to be later. It's a bit of a circus for now.'

Like his life. A juggling act. One that entailed keeping far too many balls in the air without dropping them. There was no applause for keeping them going either— just the prospect of disaster if they got dropped.

After the spooky driveway and the austere outlines of the huge, old stone farmhouse, walking into the kitchen was so far towards the other end of a welcoming spectrum that it was almost overwhelming.

A crackling open fire at one end of the room made it so warm Emma knew she'd have to take her pullover off very soon. The lights gave the oak cabinetry a golden glow and there was an amazing smell of something hot and meaty that made her mouth water. Good grief…she couldn't remember the last time she'd actually felt *hungry*.

'Look…' Poppy pointed to a fridge that was covered with pieces of paper and photographs held in place by small magnets. 'I drawed that. It's my mummy. She's got wings because she's an angel.'

'Oh?' The statement had been completely matter-of-fact but Emma wasn't sure how to take it. Was Mummy exceptionally kind or was she dead? Catherine was busy putting oven gloves on and didn't seem to have overheard the comment and she didn't like to ask Poppy. No doubt she would find out in good time.

'I drawed this one, too. It's Daddy and Bob and Benji.'

'It's very good. They all look very happy.'

Not that Emma could imagine Adam actually having such a wide grin on his face. Glancing back, she saw him standing in the doorway, all but glowering at the scene in front of him. She also saw Oliver bumping the guitar case on the flagstone floor.

'That's a bit heavy for you.' Easing out of Poppy's firm grip on her hand, Emma went to rescue the guitar. 'I'll put it over here for now, yes?'

'No,' Oliver said. 'I want to see.' With his eyebrows fiercely frowning like that, he looked remarkably similar to his father.

'It's time to eat,' Catherine told him. 'Poor Emma's been travelling all day and she must be famished. And then I'm going to show her to her room and drive all the way to Edinburgh to the airport.'

Poppy's face fell dramatically. 'But I don't want you to go, Granny. You'll miss *Christmas*.'

'No, I won't.' Catherine was opening a door on the stove that was set into an old chimney lined with blue and white tiles. She took out a cast-iron pot that looked as old as the kitchen and carried it to the table. 'They have Christmas in Canada too, you know. I'll be calling you and telling you all about your new wee cousin.'

'We can video chat.' Adam moved to the table and picked up a bread knife. He began slicing the crusty loaf on a thick wooden board. 'You'll be able to see the bairn as well.'

Poppy sniffed loudly. Emma took hold of her hand

again and bent to whisper in her ear. 'Can you show me where to sit? It's such a *big* table.'

'You can sit beside me.'

In a short space of time Emma was installed on one of the old, oak chairs beside Poppy, with Oliver and Catherine on the other side of the table. Adam was at the top. Past him, she could see the dogs stretched out in front of the fire, with her guitar case propped against the wall nearby, looking as out of place as she was.

Except, oddly, she didn't *feel* out of place at all. She looked up at the whitewashed ceiling with its dramatic dark beams, across at the pretty tiles around the stove and the cluster of antique kettles and pots on the floor beside it. The room could have been part of a museum, except that it was so alive with the feeling of family.

It wasn't just the fridge that was covered with works of art and photographs. There was a huge corkboard on the wall and a bookshelf that had framed photographs amongst the books and a shelf clearly devoted to things the children had made, like an odd-looking robot constructed out of cardboard boxes and tubes and a chunky effort in clay that could possibly represent Benji. Or maybe Daddy.

'It's only stew, I'm sorry,' Catherine said, as she ladled an aromatic mix of meat and vegetables onto Emma's plate. 'I forgot that we might be welcoming a visitor today.'

A visitor? The feeling of family was so strong Emma had forgotten that that was what she was. How could anyone not feel completely at home in here? And the food was delicious.

'This is perfect,' Emma assured Catherine. A lot better than anything she'd be able to produce in the kitchen. Oh…help… Had she really made Adam believe she could cook in that interview? Her job in the restaurant had been limited to clearing tables and washing dishes. And had Catherine made that bread herself, too? Possibly even churned the butter, she thought as she accepted the blue and white dish being passed her way by Adam.

She didn't need to cross that bridge quite yet, though. And maybe it was Catherine that Adam had inherited that fey ability to see things from. She was smiling at Emma as they all tucked into their dinners.

'I've left lots of meals in the freezer and there's a modern oven as well as the big stove, if you need it. The children get a hot lunch at school so you'll only have to cope with breakfast for most of the time.'

'Did the turkey for Christmas arrive?' Adam asked.

'Aye. It's in the freezer as well. Don't forget to take it out at least a couple of days early. Leave it in the big tub out in the dairy to thaw.'

'I don't like stew,' Oliver announced a few minutes later. 'It's got carrots in it.'

'Carrots are good for you,' Emma offered. 'They help you see in the dark.'

'I don't need to see in the dark,' Oliver said with exaggerated patience. 'I'm *asleep*.'

'If you don't eat your carrots,' Adam said calmly, 'there'll be no ice cream.'

'I don't like ice cream.'

'I do,' Poppy sighed. 'I *love* ice cream.'

'Me, too,' Emma said. She beamed at Poppy. Impossible not to fall in love with a child who was so prepared to love everything life had to offer. Poppy beamed back. Shifting her gaze back to her plate, Emma caught Adam staring at her but he quickly shifted his attention back to his son.

'No television before bed, then,' he said. 'Vegetables are important.'

Catherine stood up to start clearing plates. 'Can I leave you to do the children's pudding?' she asked Adam. 'I'll need to head away soon and I'd like to give Emma a tour of the house and show her where her room is.'

'But Emma loves ice cream, too.' The horrified look on Poppy's face at the prospect of such an unwarranted punishment for someone stole another piece of Emma's heart. Oliver might prove to be more of a challenge but she knew that she was going to love her time with Poppy.

'I'll come back,' Emma promised. 'Save me some, okay?' She looked at Oliver, who was scowling down at his plate—the only one still on the table. He was pushing slices of carrot around with his fork. 'And by then,' she added casually, 'you'll have scoffed those carrots, Ollie, and I'll be able to show you my guitar.'

A lightning-fast glance back as she left the kitchen revealed a fork laden with carrot slices making its way towards Oliver's mouth and Emma hid a smile. Maybe the little boy wouldn't be too much of a challenge after all.

The tour of the house was a whirlwind and it wasn't just the speed of viewing the more formal rooms, like the lounge and library downstairs or the rapid climb to the upper level that had taken Emma's breath away.

'How old is the house?'

'The main part dates back to the seventeenth century but there's been a lot of additions and renovations, and thank goodness for that. I'd hate to be offering you a room that didn't have an en suite bathroom.' Down the end of a wide hallway that had dozens of framed photographs displayed, Catherine opened one of the dark oak doors. 'And here it is.'

'It's gorgeous.' Emma looked around the space that

would be hers for the next few weeks. The brass bed had a pretty patchwork quilt. The fireplace was tiled in blue and white, which seemed to be a theme throughout the house, and any draught from the windows was kept at bay by the thick velvet curtains that Catherine whisked shut.

'Poppy and Ollie's rooms are next door and they have their own bathroom between them. There's a playroom on this side and down the other hallway there are a couple of guest rooms and Adam's room is at the end. Have a good explore tomorrow, when you've got some daylight.' Catherine glanced at her watch. 'I'm so sorry, but I'm going to have to dash. I need to get home and collect my suitcase.'

'Home? Don't you live here?'

'Not any more. I moved out when Adam and Tania got married. It's been a family tradition for generations that the eldest son raises his family here. I have a cottage in the village.'

So it had been a family home for generations? That would explain the astonishingly homely feel of the house. And the enormous collection of photographs. Emma followed Catherine back into the hallway. She bit her lip but her curiosity refused to subside.

'Would it be awfully rude if I asked about…Tania?'

'Of course not, pet.' Catherine stopped in her tracks, turned her head to scrutinise the gallery of photographs and then pointed. 'That's her. I think that picture was taken on their honeymoon in the Maldives.'

A stunning beach scene. An even more stunning young woman with long, blonde hair and a model's body frolicking in the surf. Laughing. The joy was unmistakeable and Emma could imagine Adam standing there with the camera, capturing such a happy moment with his new wife.

'She's beautiful.'

'Aye...' The word was a sigh. 'Poppy has the look of her, I think. Ollie's more like his dad.'

There were more photographs, of course. Emma spotted a wedding portrait, with Adam gazing adoringly at his bride. A lovely black and white image of Tania and the newborn twins and more with the babies as toddlers.

'The bairns were only three when it happened,' Catherine said softly. 'They barely remember their mother so it's good to have so many pictures for them.'

Emma swallowed hard. 'What did happen?'

'A terrible tragedy. Tania liked to do her Christmas shopping in Edinburgh and she'd stay in a B&B so she could get it all done in a couple of days. There was a fire that year and she was trapped. She didn't get burned but they said she died of smoke inhalation.'

'Right before *Christmas*? That's so sad.'

'Aye.' Catherine caught her gaze for a long moment. There was a hint of warning in her gaze. And a plea. 'You might need to be patient with Adam. It's no' an easy time of year for him.'

'I can imagine.' No wonder he seemed so terse and grumpy, Emma thought. Or that she had yet to see him smile. How hard would it be to have the whole world joyously celebrating family and times of togetherness when it marked the anniversary of losing a beautiful and beloved young wife? The mother of his children?

'But Christmas is for the bairns, isn't it?' Catherine added. 'And they're old enough to see that their Christmas is no' like all the other bairns in the village and that's no' really fair, is it?'

Emma held the older woman's gaze. 'I'll do my best to make it a special Christmas for them,' she promised.

'Aye...' Catherine patted her arm. 'I've a feeling you

might do just that. Thank you.' Her smile was poignant. 'The bairns think their mother is an angel who's still looking after them. Maybe that was why you got sent to us.'

When his mother drove away from the house on the first leg of her journey to Canada, Adam was left standing on the front steps.

Stunned.

What had just happened here?

He'd been dreading this moment for months. Ever since he had learned of his sister's due date and realised that—for the first time since Tania's death—he might have to face this Christmas without the emotional support of the most important woman in his life. And worse, that the twins would be without their beloved grandmother, who was the one who insisted on making the day as special as possible for them.

He'd expected tears. Possibly tantrums, especially from Poppy, who simply adored her gran. Oliver was just as attached, of course, but he didn't wear his heart on his sleeve like Poppy. He was more like himself, in guarding his heart and not letting others see any private misery. His children were his life—both of them—but he did worry more about Ollie. Because he knew just how much misery it was possible to hide?

But the moment had come. They'd all been out there to say goodbye to Catherine. Even the unknown quantity that was the new arrival of the temporary nanny because his mother wouldn't let her hang back from the family farewell. She'd been standing there beside the children— looking remarkably like a wayward, teenage sister— getting one of those warm hugs that Catherine was so good at. And then she'd whispered something in Ollie's ear and his little boy had given a solemn nod and turned to lead the way back inside. Poppy had jumped up and down and tugged on Emma's hand and she was bursting with excitement as she dragged Emma back up the steps.

'We're going to see the *kit-ar*,' she informed Adam as they went past. 'I *love* kit-ars.'

Benji had bounded in their wake, of course. It was Bob who was sitting by Adam's feet and he saw the dog shiver. How long had he been standing here, wondering how on earth something he'd been dreading had turned out to be so easy?

Long enough for his dog to shiver noticeably.

'Come on, then, old boy.'

Back in the warmth of the house, he pushed the heavy door closed and then he heard it.

The sound of music coming from the kitchen.

Expertly plucked guitar strings. A song being sung in a clear, sweet voice that filled the air and made it somehow more of a pleasure to breathe.

A childish song, he realised as he stepped closer to the bright glow of the kitchen door. A nonsense song with tongue-twister words about a copper coffee-pot.

And it wasn't just Emma singing. Poppy was getting the words wrong and giggling but Oliver must have learned the song at school because he was joining in part of the chorus.

Not very loudly but he knew his son's voice.

He stopped again. Puzzled.

What *was* it about this girl?

His mother had seen it instantly. Poppy was prepared to love everybody. But Ollie...?

How on earth had she put her hands on a key to that little heart so quickly?

Adam shook his head and Bob lay down and put his nose on his paws to wait.

He knew when something big was changing. And he knew that it took longer for his master to recognise any joyful possibilities that something new could offer. His job was simply to keep him company while he had a little think about it all.

CHAPTER THREE

'So Mrs McAllister's likin' Canada, then?'

'Aye.' Adam glanced over his shoulder, reaching for the file on the end of Eileen's desk, as his next patient joined him for the short walk to his consulting room. The waiting area was still full, and while the women amongst the group seemed busy with their knitting or magazines, he knew perfectly well that they'd all been discussing his business while he'd been taking Shona Legg's blood tests.

Or, to be more accurate, they'd been comparing notes on the new arrival in the village. Emma had been here for a few days now and there was nothing like a bit of new blood to stimulate opinions.

Eileen had overheard the comment by way of greeting from the elderly woman who was moving slowly beside him. She sniffed audibly.

'Don't hold wi' havin' Christmas in foreign parts,' he heard her mutter. 'It's no' natural to be away from your home.'

Adam suppressed a sigh as Miss McClintock's progress slowed even more as she turned her head. 'Canada's no' so foreign,' she informed Eileen. 'And Christmas is about people, no' places. Dr McAllister's sister's there and she's having a bairn. It's where the first Mrs McAllister *should* be.'

'Come in, Joan.' Adam closed the door firmly behind them. 'And tell me what's brought you here today.'

'I'm a bit peaky is all.'

'Oh?' Adam smiled encouragingly but his heart was sinking. It had been, ever since that reference to the first Mrs McAllister. The title had come from the need to distinguish Catherine from the new woman with the same name—Tania. This was really what that overfull waiting room was about, wasn't it? It had happened all those years ago, too, when he'd brought his new wife home from the bright lights of Edinburgh. Who knew what interesting piece of information he might let slip when faced with the relentless curiosity of people who'd known him all his life?

They loved him. He knew that. They'd been prepared to accept and admire Tania, too, despite her being a foreigner from the bright lights of Edinburgh, and the excitement that her pregnancy and the birth of the twins had generated had kept the older biddies happy for months. So had the tragedy of her death. They'd closed ranks around him now and anyone who might pose even the smallest threat was going to be regarded with deep suspicion.

How on earth was Emma coping with that side of village life?

'What sort of peaky?'

Joan McClintock removed her hat. Adam obediently took it and placed it on his desk as she began unwinding her hand-knitted scarf from around her neck.

'I don't feel quite right,' his patient said vaguely. 'A wee bit giddy in my head when I stand up sometimes.'

Adam's nod was brisk. Blood pressure first, then. Possibly an ECG to check for an arrhythmia. At the very least a review of the medications Joan was taking. It was unlikely he'd be finished within the fifteen-minute slot that Eileen would have allocated in her appointment schedule but he would have to try.

'I saw the bairns in the square yesterday,' Joan told him as he helped her off with her thick coat. 'Watching the decorations go up on the tree. It's such a blessing they don't remember, isn't it?'

'Aye.' The agreement was as terse as Adam could make it without causing offence. A warning that discussing his private life was not an option. 'No, you don't need to take off your cardigan, Joan. We can just roll up your sleeve for me to do your blood pressure.'

It *was* a blessing that his children couldn't remember the dreadful Christmas of three years ago. Had Emma been given the story in lurid detail, as she'd done her chores in the village over the last few days? December wasn't just about a season of goodwill in Braeburn. It marked the season of remembrance for Tania McAllister.

His mother was lucky she was in Canada. She was getting a reprieve from being the unspoken centre of attention when family was being celebrated. Away from a village where Christmas had a distinct flavour of being a shrine to someone who had been elevated to the status of a saint.

Dear Lord…if they only *knew* the truth…

But he hadn't known so why should they? Oh, they'd all seen how she'd escaped the village more and more often but, while eyebrows had been raised about her time away from the children, it had been accepted as part of a glamorous woman's life and it had been forgiven and forgotten after her tragic death.

What none of them knew was that she probably hadn't been alone on any of those trips away.

He'd only found out because fate had stepped in and

provided the evidence and Adam had made sure that the scandalous information had gone no further.

Maybe that was the real blessing here. That the village—and therefore his children—would never know.

It was his burden and that was only fair, wasn't it? If he'd been a better husband, Tania wouldn't have needed anyone else. And it was a burden he was getting used to carrying. In many ways it was getting easier and he could hope that some time in the future he'd be able to cope with this particular time of year. Enjoying it was too much to ever hope for but another few weeks and things could get back to normal. A normality he would never have chosen, of course, but he could live with it.

He had no choice.

'That English lassie was wi' them.' Joan only just managed to wait until Adam was removing the stethoscope from his ears. 'I hear she's made friends with Caitlin McMurray at the school?'

His grunt was intended to express a lack of interest in his temporary nanny's social life. Why did some people assume that a monosyllabic response simply needed more effort on their part?

'I hear she's been *singing*.'

'Aye.' Adam was still having difficulty getting used to the sound of Emma singing. She did it *all* the time. When she was busy with some mundane task, like doing the dishes or sorting laundry, and a session of songs with the children was already a favourite part of their evening routine. She probably thought the nursery wing was far enough away from the rest of the house for him not to notice but she was wrong. He'd heard her late last night, too, well after the children were sound asleep. Alone in her room, playing her guitar and singing softly.

It wasn't that he didn't *like* the sound. It was just…
different. Nothing like normal.

'She's no' a teacher.' Joan clicked her tongue. 'What's
she doing at the school *every* day?'

It was the tone that did it. Adam was jolted out of his
automatic defence mechanisms by the unexpected urge to
defend his new employee. 'She *has* been a music teacher
and she plays the guitar. The school's piano is apparently
broken and the children want to learn carols. Now…stand
up, please, Joan. I'm going to take your blood pressure
again to see if position makes any difference.'

Joan levered her ample frame out of the chair. 'We
knew about the piano. The committee's talking about
whether to use the hall fund to replace it, but if we don't
fix the hall it's going to get condemned and what would
we do without the village hall? Where would the children put on their Christmas play?'

Adam resorted to his customary grunt and put the ear-
pieces of his stethoscope into place to signal an end to
the conversation. As he held the disc over Joan's elbow
and pumped up the cuff, he took a quick glance at the
clock on his wall and remembered the number of people
in the waiting room.

It was going to be a long day.

The conversation stopped as soon as Emma entered the
general store that was between the greengrocer and the
bakery. She lifted her chin and put on her brightest smile.

'Good morning. I'm looking for some coloured paper.
Do you have the kind that's sticky on the back?'

The blank stare made Emma reconsider her decision
to shop in the village instead of driving for half an hour
to get to the nearest larger town. It wasn't easy to keep
the smile on her face.

'I want to make paper chains,' she explained. 'For Christmas decorations.'

The women exchanged heavily significant glances.

'*Christmas* decorations?' one of them murmured. 'In Dr McAllister's hoose?'

The subtext was in capital letters. You couldn't really celebrate Christmas in the McAllister house. Not without being duly reluctant anyway. Even the children were all too aware of that and it wasn't fair. She'd taken them to watch the big tree in the square being decorated yesterday and Poppy's eyes had been huge.

'I *love* Christmas trees,' she'd whispered. 'They're so *pretty*.'

'We'll make your Christmas tree just as pretty at home, you'll see.'

'We don't have a tree at home,' Oliver had said. 'Gran says it's because it makes Dad sad.'

'It makes me sad,' Poppy had said, '*not* having a tree.'

Emma had lain awake last night, mulling this over. She was here for the children, wasn't she? And she was here for Christmas.

And Christmas was for children.

It was a no-brainer, really. Surely she could find a way to persuade the taciturn Dr McAllister to put up with a few decorations? When Catherine had called from Canada early that morning to talk to the children before they went off to school, Emma had gathered her courage and asked quietly if it would be such a terrible thing to do.

'It would be the best thing to do,' Catherine had assured her. 'It's no guid for anyone, being stuck in the past. I've tried but...' The sigh said it all. 'Maybe *you'll* succeed, pet. He can't afford to chase you away, can he? Not before Christmas, anyway.'

The tone that suggested it wouldn't be an easy task

was being heavily underlined by the shocked look these women were now sharing.

'It's for Poppy and Oliver,' Emma said firmly. 'They've been making decorations at school and they want to make some at home, too. Paper chains are what I always made when I was their age.'

The mention of the children made one of the women nod. 'Aye,' she sighed. 'It should be all about the bairns, shouldn't it?'

'The paper's over yon,' the shopkeeper told Emma. 'Beside the magazines.'

The conversation didn't stop this time as she returned to the counter.

'Poor man,' one was saying. 'To lose the love of his life so young.'

'Like a princess, she was,' another agreed. 'Always so well dressed.'

Emma felt the collective scrutiny of her jeans and oversized jumper beneath her puffy anorak and she was perversely delighted that she was wearing her Tibetan knitted hat with its rainbow stripes and ear covers that trailed into long tails she hadn't bothered tying. That would really give them something to disapprove of at length as soon as she went out the door.

Her bravado faded as she picked up the guitar case she'd left by the umbrella stand at the shop door and went out into the chilly, grey afternoon, however. If making a paper chain or two was such a big deal, maybe she was only going to make things worse? How happy would the children be if their father was even more upset by someone who wasn't prepared to spend Christmas in a kind of muted mourning?

The Christmas tree in the square had taken days to decorate but it was looking magnificent now, with big, coloured lights and enormous red and silver baubles. Despite the cold, Emma perched on a bench near the church. She had half an hour before she was due at school. Checking her watch, she made a quick calculation. They were about eight hours behind Californian time and that meant that Sharon was probably at home. She hit the speed dial.

'Emma...I was just thinking about you. Is it snowing in Scotland?'

'Feels like it could be any second. I'm in the village square and it's absolutely *freezing*.'

'Ohh...I'm homesick. It's too warm to be Christmastime here. It's just *wrong*. But...you shouldn't be sitting out in the cold. Go and find somewhere warm, for heaven's sake. You have to take care of yourself.'

'I'm fine. It's too cold for bugs to survive here and my immune system is pretty much back to full power. I'm just killing some time before I go to the school for carol practice.'

Sharon laughed. 'I got your email. I can't believe you've got involved with village life that fast. No...on second thoughts, it doesn't surprise me at all. You'll be starring in the Christmas pantomime by next week.'

'No. That's Ollie and Poppy. They've been chosen to be Joseph and Mary for the school nativity play. They're so excited. I'm going to have to make costumes for them.'

'Uh-oh... Do they know you can't sew?'

Emma laughed. 'No. They don't even know I can't cook yet. Their gran left so much food in the freezer I've been able to keep my lack of talent well hidden.'

'Imagine if you gave the only doctor in town food poisoning?'

'Hey...that only happened once. I give chicken a wide berth now.'

'Good thinking. He wouldn't be happy.'

'He's not happy anyway. Do you know I haven't seen him smile once yet?'

'He's Scottish. He's supposed to be dour.'

'He still wears his wedding ring and it's three years since his wife died.'

'Hmm. He must have loved her.'

'Who wouldn't? From what I've heard, she was either a princess, an angel or some kind of saint.'

'Nobody's that perfect. People just forget the bad stuff when they're dead.'

Emma smiled but couldn't help wondering if Sharon would forget about the food poisoning incident if…

'Oh, my God…what *is* that horrendous noise?'

Laughter chased away the dark thought. 'There's an old guy in a kilt near the Christmas tree. He's warming up his bagpipes.'

'What? Sounds like a tribe of donkeys braying.'

'No. That's even worse. You should hear Jemima waking us all up in the mornings. She's very cute but remind me that I never want a donkey as a pet in the future, will you?'

'What was that? I can hardly hear you.'

'I'd better go, Sharon. I'm due at school. Talk soon. Love you.'

The piper was playing a real tune by the time Emma tucked her phone into her pocket and, instead of the brisk walk she had intended to get her circulation moving again, she sat there and listened for a minute.

It was such an evocative sound with a haunting edge that was a song of what…courage? Loneliness?

Maybe it was just the quintessential Scottishness of it but it made her think of Adam McAllister.

Did he ever wear a kilt?

The notion gave her an odd curl somewhere deep in her belly.

What *was* it about men in kilts that could be such a sexy image?

Or was it the image of Adam in the attire that was making her feel a little odd?

It was easy to dismiss such a ridiculous idea because something else was happening in her head.

Or maybe her heart.

Perhaps it was the Christmas tree she was looking at in combination with the haunting music. Or maybe it had something to do with that moment in her phone call to Sharon when she'd wondered if her friend would only remember the good things.

Whatever it was, Emma was facing the realisation that this could possibly be the last Christmas she would ever have.

And she was going to be sharing it with children who had no memory of what a happy, family Christmas should be all about.

With a man who couldn't see how precious life was and how you had to catch joy—not shut it out or allow it to be dimmed by shadows.

The fey notion that fate had sent her here for a reason suddenly made sense. If this was going to be her last Christmas, how lucky was she that she could share it with Poppy and Oliver?

She was going to make this the *best* Christmas ever.

Starting with paper chains.

CHAPTER FOUR

FLIGHTS OF FANCY first thing in the morning were a bit much but Emma seemed to have no control over this one.

Here she was, standing by the kitchen bench, breaking eggs, and a single glance over her shoulder to where the man of the house was having his breakfast had been enough to trigger it.

She could see Adam McAllister wearing a kilt. With his hair even longer than the current shaggy style so that dark, tangled waves kissed his shoulders. Standing in solitary splendour on the top of a hill, with a set of bagpipes tucked under his arm, offering a mournful lament to the universe. It was almost enough to bring a tear to her eyes. She certainly had to stifle a sigh.

In fact, Adam was wearing a dark jumper over his shirt and tie, buttering his toast and adding marmalade, just like any normal mortal. There was no excuse for the words that popped out of Emma's mouth.

'Is there a McAllister tartan?'

'What?' Adam's hand stopped halfway towards his mug of tea. He sounded both impatient and bewildered.

Emma made herself walk to the fridge to get some milk for the eggs but she couldn't look at Adam. She'd woken up a little nervous that this was the start of the weekend and she'd be seeing a lot more of the children's father. She'd been hoping to impress him by how well she'd settled into this new job but she'd obviously annoyed him by asking a stupid question.

'It's just that I saw a man playing the bagpipes in the village yesterday and he was wearing a kilt. I know that the colours and patterns vary according to clan and I just wondered...' Oh, help. Now she was prattling on. 'If, you know, you had one for your family.'

'Of course we do.'

'Oh...' Emma waited but that seemed to be the end to the conversation. 'That's nice.' She poured milk into the bowl of eggs and started whisking them. The silence stretched on.

'We're a branch of Clan Donald,' Adam said, with an air of having realised he might have been rude in giving such a terse response. 'The tartan's red and green with white stripes and a little bit of royal blue.'

'Sounds lovely.' Emma pressed her lips together but the question refused to stay unspoken. 'Do you ever wear a kilt?'

'Only for weddings.' She could feel Adam glaring at her back. 'And funerals.'

Oh...*man*. She took a deep breath. This was going to be a long weekend. 'Would you like some scrambled eggs? I'm making them for Poppy and Ollie.'

'No.' Adam's chair scraped as he pushed it back. 'I'm due at the medical centre. We have a Saturday morning clinic until eleven and then I've got my house calls to make.' Reaching for the crust of toast he'd left on his plate, Adam divided it and gave a piece to each of the dogs, who were flanking his chair. The action was as automatic as picking up his napkin to wipe his mouth and it made Emma feel better.

There *was* kindness lurking under that gruff exterior, wasn't there?

She almost changed her mind as he went to the kitchen door and raised his voice.

'Poppy—are you out of those pyjamas yet? Oliver—hurry up and find your chanter and don't forget your music book this time.'

He turned back to pick up the coat draped over the arm of the old couch near the fire. 'Do you know where you're taking them?'

'Yes.' Emma's nod was confident. 'I drop Ollie at Mr McTavish's house at nine o'clock, take Poppy to her dance class at the hall for nine-thirty, go back to get Ollie at ten and we pick up Poppy at ten-thirty.'

Adam gave a single nod. 'Good.'

'I thought we'd go into the village after that. We can see if they've finished decorating the big tree and get some fresh bread to go with our soup for lunch. Will you be back by then?'

'I don't know.' In his coat now, Adam reached for the leather doctor's bag that had probably been his father's before him. 'If I am, you can have the afternoon off. And tomorrow, of course, being Sunday.'

'But what would you do with the children if you got a call?'

'They come in the car with me. They're used to it.'

'I don't need a day off,' Emma told him. 'I'm loving being with the children.'

Adam paused en route to the door and the look Emma received was one of surprise. Had she sounded too enthusiastic perhaps?

Needy even?

Or maybe he thought it was some sort of rebuke directed at how little time he seemed to spend with his children.

Whatever was going on behind that dark, unreadable gaze, the eye contact made Emma's heart skip a beat. How could just a look feel like a physical touch?

It went on for long enough to make her start feeling a little peculiar and maybe he would have held her gaze even longer because Emma found herself unable to look away, but then the children burst into the room. Ollie had an instrument that looked like a recorder in one hand and a very dog-eared book in the other.

'I found them, Dad. They were under my bed.'

Poppy was right behind him. 'And I'm all dressed now. I just need Emma to do my hair.' Her face fell when she saw the bag in her father's hand. 'Are you going out now?'

'You know I have to work on Saturday mornings, love.'

Emma's gaze had been drawn straight back to Adam's face so she could see the softening as he looked down at his children. There was even a curl to his mouth that most would probably label as a smile but it wasn't a *real* smile. Had his children ever seen his eyes crinkle with happiness or basked in the joy of hearing him laugh aloud?

'I'll be back this afternoon,' he said. 'We can take the dogs for a walk if it stops raining and see if there's enough ice on the pond to go skating.'

His son's hair got ruffled and Poppy got a kiss on the top of her head and then he was gone. The children—and the dogs—were left staring forlornly after him.

'Who wants eggs?' Emma asked brightly.

'Me. I *love* eggs.' Poppy climbed up onto a chair.

'I don't.' Oliver kicked his chair leg before sitting down. 'I think they're *icky*.'

'Icky eggs.' Poppy giggled but then cast a doubtful look towards the pan Emma was stirring.

'That's only because you haven't tried my special scrambled eggs,' Emma said firmly. 'They're from your very own hens and they look yummy. I'm going to have some too and then we're going to get our skates on and get you to your classes on time.'

Poppy frowned. 'I don't think I can dance with my skates on.'

Emma laughed. 'It means that we need to be quick.' She put a plate of scrambled eggs in front of Poppy. 'To go fast, like we're pretending to be on skates.'

'I love skating.' Poppy picked up her fork. 'I hope the pond is all freezed up. Will you come and have a look on our walk, too, Emma?'

The wide-eyed, hopeful look that accompanied the invitation was irresistible but Emma rapidly replayed Adam's words in her head. He'd offered to take the children for a walk. He'd told her she could have the afternoon off. That added up to him wanting time alone with his children, didn't it?

'I might have some things I need to do,' she told Poppy. 'But you can tell me all about it later.'

Adam wasn't home by the time the soup was hot and the crusty loaf of bread had been sliced and buttered.

'I don't think we'll wait,' Emma decided. 'I can leave some soup on the stove to stay hot for Daddy and we'll save him lots of bread.'

'And a chocolate?'

'Does Daddy like chocolate?'

'Mmm.' Poppy nodded her head enthusiastically but then frowned. 'Not as much as me.'

Emma eyed the small bowl on the table. 'You didn't open too many doors on your calendar, did you?'

Poppy shook her head. 'That's Ollie's chocolates too. Is there really one behind every door until it gets to Christmas?'

'Sure is. Have you guys never had an Advent calendar before?'

Poppy shook her head again. 'Jeannie told me about them at school but I didn't believe her.'

A momentary doubt surfaced as Emma looked at the two Advent calendars now pinned to the bottom of the big corkboard, within easy reach of the children. Surely Adam wouldn't object to them having the excitement of opening the doors to find the treat and the tiny Christmassy picture every morning?

'Ollie? You can stop practising now. Come and have lunch.'

'I'm going to wait for Dad.'

'But we don't know how long he'll be. You must be hungry.'

Sitting on the sofa, Oliver shook his head and kept blowing on his chanter, laboriously changing his finger positions over the holes. The noise was terrible. No wonder the dogs were looking unhappy.

'Tell you what…' Emma had to raise her voice to be heard over the shrill notes. 'Why don't you have a little bit now and then some more when Dad gets home?'

Oliver appeared not to have heard the suggestion but when the telephone rang he dropped his chanter and ran to answer it. He came back scowling. 'Dad says Mrs Jessop is having her baby and it's coming too early so he has to stay and look after her until the ambulance comes and he might have to go into the hospital with her, too. He might not be home till teatime.'

'Oh...' Emma's heart gave a squeeze at the small boy's obvious disappointment. 'We'll just have to find something fun to do until then, won't we?'

Oliver's scowl deepened.

Emma tried hard to keep the children amused and cheer Oliver up. They all put wellies and coats on and took some carrots out for Jemima the donkey, who was very happy to have visitors. Emma scratched her woolly head and stroked the extraordinary ears.

'She has beautiful eyes.'

'She's really clever,' Oliver said. 'She can undo knots. Dad says it's no use ever tying her up.'

Poppy was being nuzzled gently.

'She's kissing me, Emma. See? She loves me. She 'specially loves it when I ride her.'

'Really? Does she have a saddle?'

'You don't need one,' Oliver told her. 'There's lots of fluff to hang onto and she never goes fast.'

'How does she know where to go?'

'She follows *me*,' Oliver said. He stood a little taller. 'That's why she's so good at undoing knots. She doesn't like being tied up because she wants to follow me. Jemima loves me, too.'

'She's quiet now,' Emma observed. 'She's pretty loud in the mornings, isn't she?'

'That's because she's lonely,' Poppy said sadly. 'Donkeys need to have a friend.'

'Can we go and look at the pond now?'

'Do you know where it is, Ollie?'

'Up there.' His arm waved vaguely towards the wooded hill behind the house that separated the garden from surrounding farmland. 'Somewhere.'

'Hmm.' It was tempting to take the children and dogs off for a walk but Emma had a sudden vision of them all getting lost in the Scottish highlands. She could imagine the activation of the local search and rescue team as the snow started falling thickly and what Adam's face would be like if she put his children into such danger.

Maybe it was fortunate that the leaden sky overhead decided to release the first fat raindrops on top of them.

'Let's get Jemima tucked up into her nice warm stable. I've got something special we can do inside.'

'What?'

'It's a surprise.'

It was certainly Oliver that the donkey was willing to follow. He didn't even need to hang onto her halter as he led her into the straw-covered stable. They closed the bottom half of the door so she could see out but the mournful braying started even before they got back to the house.

'She's lonely again,' Poppy said. Her bottom lip quivered.

'Oh…look.' Emma wanted to distract Poppy. 'That's a holly hedge. Let's pick some.'

'Why?'

'Because it's what you do at Christmas. We need branches that have lots of lovely red berries. Let's see how quickly we can find some and get inside before it really starts raining.'

The rain was pouring down by the time they reached the warmth of the kitchen again. The dogs left muddy paw prints over the flagstone floor and curled up close to the fire that Emma stoked. She cleared the table and produced the packets of coloured paper she had purchased in the village the day before and showed them how to cut strips and make interlocking loops by sticking the ends together.

'Do lots of different colours,' she said. 'And make them really long. I'll find something to stick them up with and we'll make the kitchen so pretty it will be a lovely surprise for when Daddy gets home.'

The task was a novelty that the children loved. The strips were a bit wobbly and the loops a variety of sizes but it didn't detract from the overall effect as the simple decorations grew. Emma cleaned up the lunch dishes and found a big bowl to arrange the holly branches in. She sang the Christmas carol the children had never heard about the little donkey and Poppy made her sing it again and again as she tried to learn the words.

Then she searched cluttered drawers until she found some drawing pins and tape that she could use to hang the paper chains. This required some effort, moving the table and then standing on a chair on top of it but by the time daylight had faded completely they were able to stand back and admire the team effort.

Rainbow chains linked all four corners of the room, dipping between the beams to give graceful curves to the lines. The whitewashed ceiling made the colours seem even brighter and the transformation from ordinary to festive was very gratifying. Who wouldn't love it?

The sound of singing was the last thing Adam needed when he stepped into his home after a long and difficult afternoon. The happy sound was totally inappropriate when he'd just left people who were suffering—like poor Aimee Jessop, who looked like she might lose yet another bairn.

The clock had stopped, he noted. Because he'd forgotten to wind it.

At least Bob wasn't limping as much but it had been Emma who had decided to take him to the vet to have his dressing changed and receive instructions on how to care for the dog. Had Jim, the vet, made some comment about how it was just as well it wasn't going to be left entirely in Adam's hands?

And it had been Emma who'd made him feel like he wasn't doing enough for his children, too. The way she'd said how much she loved being with them this morning. He loved being with them, too, but how many others would realise that?

He'd promised to spend the afternoon with them today and look what had happened.

A premature labour at only twenty-seven weeks for poor Aimee. Four weeks longer than the previous two pregnancies and she'd really begun to hope that this time she would get to take her baby home. He'd tried to keep her calm until the ambulance arrived and he couldn't have let her go to the hospital alone. Not when her husband was out on the oil rig for another two weeks.

Not even noticing the muddy streak Benji's paw left on his trousers, Adam kept moving. Maybe a wee dram of whisky before his tea would help. And some time with the children. He could read them a story before bed.

The words of the song were audible now. "'Little donkey, little donkey, on the dusty road…'"

Maybe the children would prefer to hear songs than a story.

Adam stepped into the kitchen. He was expecting warmth and the smell of hot food. The loving greeting his children always gave him and the prospect of winding down in the comfort of his favourite part of his house. He wasn't expecting to be hit in the face with a blinding kaleidoscope of colours.

'What in heaven's name is *going on* in here?'

'*Daddy…*' Poppy flung her arms around his legs. 'We've made decorations. Aren't they bee-*yoot*-i-ful?'

Adam took another upward glance at the desecration of the ancient, oak beams.

'And we've learned a song all about Jemima.'

'It's not about Jemima.' Oliver was right beside his sister now. 'It's about another donkey. The one that Mary was riding to get to Bethlehem.'

Christmas again. How did it manage to accentuate the worst of life in so many ways? Impossible not to think about a donkey carrying the pregnant Mary. With a full-term pregnancy that everybody knew ended up with a healthy baby, despite less than adequate birthing facilities. Unlike poor Aimee who had access to the best of modern care but now had a scrap of a bairn who was on life support in a neonatal intensive care unit in Edinburgh.

Adam tried to push the concern away. To focus on his own healthy children. Tried to centre himself by a glance around the room below ceiling level. At least that looked relatively normal. Or did it?

'*What*…' he actually had to swallow before he could find any more words '…are *those*?'

The children had fallen strangely silent. Even Poppy, who could never be called a quiet child. It was Emma who answered.

'They're Advent calendars. You get to open a little door every day until Christmas Eve and there's a new picture and a little chocolate. Very little and the children haven't eaten them all from the doors that already needed to be opened. They saved them. For *you*.'

She sounded nervous, Adam realised. He looked over the twins' heads and looked at her properly for the first time since he'd come into the room. He still hadn't got used to the way she looked, with that air of being a stray gypsy waif, but he was certainly letting go of the idea that she could be unreliable or unable to commit to anything. She'd thrown herself into being his children's nanny with her heart and soul, hadn't she? They loved her.

And she loved them. The way she'd said how much she loved being with them this morning had touched his heart in the way that only total honesty could.

And now she was looking at him with eyes that looked too large for her thin face. With a glow that was telling him that she was doing this to make his children happy.

Because she already loved them.

And because it was Christmastime.

There was a hopeful expression in those eyes, too, that was a plea that he wouldn't spoil it all by being cross.

He found himself unable to look away. Adam got a sudden vision of what it would be like to be seeing himself through her eyes and he didn't like what he saw. He forced a smile to his lips as he managed to break the eye contact with Emma.

'As long as you don't eat too much chocolate before dinner.' He looked up again. 'I don't think I've ever seen such long paper chains. You must have been busy all day.'

'I did my practice, too. D'you want to hear what I learned today, Dad?'

'Aye. Let me get my coat off, son. And I need a wee something to drink.'

He glanced across at Emma, feeling like he should apologise, although he wasn't quite sure why. 'D'you drink whisky, Emma?'

She shook her head but smiled. 'Let me find one for you while you listen to Ollie's new tune. You've had a long day. Dinner will ready in no time.'

There was no recrimination in her tone that she'd been left with the children all afternoon and that they'd been left without their promised walk or time with their father. No… Both the tone and the way she was looking at him gave him the odd feeling that she knew exactly how hard his day had been. He didn't have to say anything about what had happened but she was still willing to try and make it better.

Even more oddly, it *was* starting to feel better. He could almost dismiss the edge of panic at seeing how Christmas was invading his house again. Maybe that was because the decorations were so obviously made by children with their wobbly shapes and sizes. Tania might have gone overboard with decorations but she would never have tolerated something so far less than perfect. Even the bunch of holly on the table was real instead of a perfect, plastic replica.

This was different. This was Emma, not Tania. Couldn't be more different, in fact. Maybe it would even be okay.

'Thank you.' It felt like the first time Adam had ever smiled at Emma but surely that wasn't the case?

Maybe it was because he'd never seen *her* smile quite like that. A slow, delighted curl to her mouth that lit up her face and gave her a faint flush of colour on those pale cheeks.

She was pretty, he realised. Not flaky looking at all. Too young for her years, still, and too thin, but…yes… pretty.

Beautiful even.

CHAPTER FIVE

EMMA HAD A lot of time to herself on Sunday because Adam didn't get called out, although he seemed to spend a lot of time on the phone and she overheard a snatch of conversation about a sick baby who was in Intensive Care. The children—and the dogs—got their long walk to see whether the pond was frozen and Emma was glad of the time on her own.

She sat in her room, with her laptop and her guitar, working on her Christmas gift for Sharon. She was writing a song about friendship and the strength it could give someone to get through hard times, and she intended to record it as a background to a slide show of all the best photos she and Sharon had taken over the last few years. She might even use the very private ones—like the one in her hospital bed where she'd been so swollen by the steroids she'd been taking and completely bald from the chemo. Sharon had insisted she needed a photo so that Emma would be able to look back and see how far she'd come and then she'd said something about eggheads and made Emma laugh, and that was the moment she'd captured.

She'd been so right. It was hard to believe how far she'd come. And maybe—Emma squeezed her eyes tightly shut for a heartbeat—she would be able to look back from the distance of many more years. But if she couldn't, Sharon would have this gift from her heart for ever.

Back in the routine of the school week again, Emma was delighted to feel so at home with the routine of her new job. She was loving her time at the school, helping with the music classes, and the new friendship with the junior-school teacher, Caitlin, promised to be something special.

It was a bonus that Oliver took so long to find everything he needed to take home after school because it gave the young women a few minutes extra to chat.

'I was telling Moira Findlay that you have one of the most amazing voices I've ever heard,' Caitlin confessed on Monday afternoon. 'She said they might consider offering you an invitation to join the village choir.'

Emma grinned. 'I take it that's a huge honour?'

'You'd better believe it. Normally you have to be second-generation Braeburn, at the very least.'

'Did you tell her I'm only here till Adam's mother gets back?'

'No.' Caitlin's face fell. 'I'm kind of hoping you'll fall in love with the place and decide to stay. He's still going to need a nanny, isn't he, and the last few have been disasters—especially that Kylie, who was far more interested in her boyfriend than the children.'

Emma backed away from the conversation fast. 'My plans are totally up in the air for next year. I couldn't commit to anything and Adam hasn't mentioned the possibility, either. I...'

The urge to say something more was strong but this wasn't the time or place. Caitlin must have sensed something big but her curious glance lasted only a moment. Poppy was tugging on Emma's hand.

'Sing Miss McMurray the new song, Emma. The Christmas one.'

'We've got lots of carols we're learning already, Poppy,' Caitlin said.

'But this is Jemima's song. About Mary.'

'"Little Donkey",' Emma supplied.

'Oh…' Caitlin's eyes shone. 'That's one of my all-time *favourite* Christmas songs. How could I have forgotten it?' She began to hum but then stopped. 'That's the chorus. How does it start again?'

Emma could see that Oliver had been totally distracted from finding his reading book by watching the goldfish in their bowl on the science table so she sang the first few lines about the little donkey on the dusty road, plodding on with its precious load.

Poppy beamed and Caitlin sighed happily. 'Imagine our play with our Mary coming in on a donkey with Joseph leading her, and all the children singing that.'

'I'm Mary,' Poppy reminded her.

'I know, pet.' Caitlin patted her head.

'And I've *got* a donkey.'

'I know that, too. But Jemima's a *real* donkey. We can't use her in our play.'

'Why not?' Emma was caught by the image. Adam would be there in the audience, wouldn't he? How amazing would that be, to see his two children and their pet creating Christmas magic for the whole village? She could take photos and give them a new memory that would always remind them of a joyous moment.

Caitlin was staring at her as if she had lost her mind.

'She's a very good donkey,' Emma continued. 'And Poppy's used to riding her.' From the corner of her eye she noted that Oliver had stopped watching the fish and was now watching them. 'Would she still follow you in a strange place, Ollie? Would you be able to lead her?'

Oliver scowled at her. ''Course I would.'

'They could just come down the centre aisle and then the children could take their place on the stage and someone could take Jemima out the side door.'

'Ohh…' Caitlin was clearly completely captured. 'How would we get her to the hall, though?'

That was a problem. 'It *is* too far to walk,' Emma agreed.

'My brother's girlfriend's aunt runs a donkey sanctuary not far from here,' Caitlin said thoughtfully. 'I wonder if we could borrow a float?'

Poppy was bouncing up and down on her toes. 'Hooray…Jemima's going to be in our play.'

'Hang on,' her teacher warned. 'Don't get too excited. And don't tell anybody else about it. We'll have to get all sorts of permission, like from the hall committee and from your daddy.'

The bright glow of the idea dimmed for Emma. Neither authority was likely to be too enthusiastic about this inspiration but she suspected Adam would be the hardest to convince.

But he was okay with the paper chains now, wasn't he? And the Advent calendars and the holly? Maybe another small push forward would help get him into feeling the goodwill of the season more. When they passed a man selling Christmas trees off the back of a lorry on their way home, Emma stamped on the brakes.

'I think we need a tree,' she said aloud. 'What do you think, kidlets?'

The twins were silent.

'We could put it in the big living room,' Emma suggested. 'And we could make decorations for it. And then your presents can go underneath it on Christmas Eve. Is that what you usually do?'

'We don't have a tree.' Poppy's voice was very small. 'We only go and see the tree by the church and the one in Gran's house.'

A glance in the rear-view mirror revealed an expression on Oliver's face rather like the one that had been on Caitlin's when Emma had suggested adding Jemima to the junior school's play. As if she was completely crazy.

'Maybe that's because Daddy gets too busy at Christmastime. Would you like to have a tree, Poppy?'

Poppy thought about this for a long moment. 'Jeannie has her very own tree.'

'So does Jamie,' Oliver said. 'And Ben and…and *everybody.*'

Emma channelled Catherine McAllister. It was up to her to make Christmas happen for these children, even if the thought of the repercussions of this step were more than a little scary.

'Right, then.' She reached for her wallet. 'Come on. You can help me choose the *best* one.'

'No.'

'But, Daddy…I *want* Jemima to be in our play. *Please…*'

'*No.*' Adam's fork clattered against his plate in the silence that followed the resoundingly negative response.

It was just as well that Emma had waited until dinner was almost finished before broaching the subject of including the largest family pet in the nativity play. Her appetite evaporated in the face of the atmosphere that instantly filled the McAllister kitchen—her favourite room in this grand old house. That single word had somehow created an impenetrable barrier and Adam was clearly angry. Was he even tasting the casserole he was forking into his mouth?

The last of the wonderful meals Catherine had left in the freezer, Emma had noted with some alarm. She would have to cook the evening meals herself from now on.

The children began simply pushing pieces of food around their plates with as little enthusiasm as Emma.

'Eat your dinner,' Adam ordered, 'or there'll be no ice cream.'

'I don't *want* ice cream.' Poppy's voice wobbled. 'I *want...*'

No, Emma begged silently. Don't say it.

'I want Jemima to be in our play.'

Adam dropped his cutlery and his chair scraped back with a screech that made Emma flinch.

'It's the most ridiculous idea I've ever heard,' he snapped. 'And it's *not* going to happen. I don't want to hear another word about it.' The stern glare Poppy was being subjected to was transferred to Oliver. 'From *either* of you.'

Then it was Emma's turn to get the look. 'I expect this was *your* idea in the first place?'

For a heartbeat she felt frightened. It wasn't just about potentially getting fired from a job she was coming to love far more than she'd expected. It was more about the glimpse into what Adam McAllister would be like if he lost control. She was sensing the depth of emotion hidden away in this man for the first time and who knew what might happen if it broke through those rigid, self-imposed constraints?

But then Emma was aware of something she rarely felt.

Anger.

She could see that the children really *were* frightened.

Sitting there, like small statues, with pale faces and probably holding their breath. Scared that their daddy didn't love them any more because they'd done something bad.

Was it so bad to dream of doing something a bit out of the ordinary? Okay…a lot out of the ordinary, but this was about *Christmas*, wasn't it? About making a little bit of magic?

So she held Adam's angry glare and lifted her chin.

'Yes,' she said clearly. 'It *was* my idea. And Caitlin McMurray loved it. She said she'd talk to the hall committee about getting permission and that she could probably arrange transport to get Jemima into the village for the evening.'

Adam was on his feet now. He crumpled his serviette into a ball and threw it down beside his unfinished plate of food.

'Have you seen the state of the village hall? It's crumbling inside. The floorboards all need replacing. Quite apart from the public-health issues of an animal needing to relieve itself indoors, there would be the danger of the floor giving way. Imagine the panic that would create? Not only could Jemima get injured but so could anybody who was unfortunate enough to be sitting anywhere nearby. Like my *children*. You're suggesting that I allow you to put them in danger for the sake of a school *play*?'

'It's a *Christmas* play.' Emma was not going to let her voice wobble like Poppy's had but it was a close call. 'It's special.'

'*Ach*…' Adam turned and strode towards the door. 'I'm going to find somewhere I can get away from this nonsense. And I don't want to hear anything more about it. From *any* of you.'

Bob followed his master from the kitchen but his head

was hanging low. Benji started to follow Bob but then stopped and slowly slunk back beneath the kitchen table.

Emma swallowed a gulp. She reached out with one hand to squeeze Poppy's hand. She would have squeezed Oliver's too, but he promptly put both his hands in his lap to avoid her touch.

'It's okay,' she told them with as much confidence as she could muster. 'Daddy just needs time to get used to the idea. He's a little bit cross but he'll get over it, you'll see.' She found a smile. 'Why don't we all have some ice cream?'

'We're not allowed,' Oliver informed her. 'We haven't eaten all our vegetables.'

'I'll bet Benji would eat them if we put them in *his* dish.'

The children looked astonished. Was an adult actually suggesting something naughty?

It wasn't the first time that Emma had been struck by how like his father Oliver was. He was deep, this little boy, and there was a sadness in him that shouldn't be there. It made her heart ache.

'Sometimes,' she said softly, 'we all need a cuddle. And having a treat like ice cream—it kind of gives us a cuddle from the inside and makes us feel better. A tummy cuddle.'

Poppy climbed off her chair and onto Emma's lap. She wound her skinny arms around Emma's neck and buried her face on her shoulder. Emma happily gathered the little girl closer and rocked her a little as she cuddled her. She held out her other arm in an invitation for Oliver to join them but he stayed where he was with his head bent as if he was staring at his hands.

They heard the roar from Adam all the way from the living room. Oh…dear Lord…Emma had forgotten the tree they'd installed in there as soon as they'd got home, thanks to the clever stand the Christmas-tree man had sold her along with the spruce the children had declared the best.

They could hear the furious footfalls as he came storming back into the kitchen.

'Whose idea was *that*, as if I couldn't guess?'

It was Emma receiving the full force of the glare this time.

'It has to stop, do you hear me? I won't have it.' Adam didn't have to reach far above his head to grab hold of one of the paper chains. And it didn't take much of a tug to have it break and drift down in pieces.

'We don't do Christmas.' He wasn't shouting but the quiet words were chillingly final. 'Not in this house.'

Poppy burst into tears. Oliver was staring at the falling paper chains and Emma just knew she was going to see this staunch little boy cry for the first time, too. But the sound that came out of his mouth was more like a cry of fear.

'*Daddy...*' His pointing was urgent and Emma turned her head automatically, in time to see the flames from the paper chain that had landed on top of the stove.

With a vehement curse Adam flung himself towards that side of the kitchen. He grabbed a tea towel, put it under the cold tap and then covered the pile of burning paper. It was all over in seconds.

Except that it wasn't over. Both the children were sobbing and this time Oliver had no objection when Emma gathered him under her free arm and took both children out of the kitchen and away from their father.

They were still sobbing by the time she'd got them bathed and into bed. Poppy fell asleep almost instantly, totally worn out by her misery. When Emma went back to check on Oliver again, she found he was also asleep—a tight ball of child entirely covered by bedding, with only his nose poking out. She bent and kissed the cold little nose.

'It'll be okay,' she whispered, just in case he wasn't really asleep. 'I promise.'

She would just have to make it okay, she decided as she forced herself to go back downstairs instead of going to hide in her room, which was what she would have preferred.

Somehow she would have to put things right.

Adam didn't hear Emma coming down the stairs but he knew she was on her way by the subtle change in the dogs. The way they pricked their ears and Benji's tail made an almost apologetic sweep of the tiles that he couldn't suppress.

He didn't look up, however, so he was still sitting there at the table with his forehead resting on one hand and a whisky glass encircled by the other as she came into the kitchen. He hadn't cleaned up the mess of charred paper yet and all he'd done with the plates of half-eaten food had been to push them to one side to make room for the whisky decanter and two glasses.

Two glasses?

Well…he had to start somewhere, didn't he?

'I'm sorry.' It was harder than he'd expected to get the words out. A shame it made it sound like he didn't really mean it but he did. He was absolutely appalled at how he'd behaved. And in front of the *children*…

He shoved the empty glass towards the closest chair at his end of the table. 'Help yourself.'

She probably didn't even drink whisky, he thought, as he remembered her refusal the other night. The night when he'd had the impression that she understood exactly how he was feeling.

Could he make her understand *this*?

The fact that she sat down in the chair and then reached to pull the stopper out of the decanter gave him a glimmer of hope. At least she was prepared to listen. He waited until he'd heard her pour herself a dram and then the clink of the stopper going back. He still couldn't look up to meet her gaze, however.

'It was the tree,' he said. 'It was in the same place. *Exactly the* same place.'

There. He'd said it. Only maybe it wasn't enough because all he got back was an expectant silence. He risked a glance up from the amber liquid he was swirling in the bottom of his glass.

Blue eyes, she had. With a hint of grey, like the sea when there was a storm on the horizon. Right now they looked as big as oceans, too. She looked as though she could already see all she needed to know but she wanted to hear the words as well.

Adam took a sip of the warmed whisky and felt the fire trickle down his gullet.

'The tree was right there beside the fire,' he said finally. 'When I got back home on Christmas Eve. It was covered with all its decorations and the lights were still flashing as though nothing had happened. All the presents were underneath, waiting for the bairns in the morning.'

Still Emma said nothing.

'I'd had to go all the way to Edinburgh,' Adam continued. 'To identify Tania's body. I'd been thinking all the way that she would be terribly burned and it would be the worst thing I'd ever seen but there wasn't a mark on her, apart from the soot in her hair and around her nose and mouth.'

It had still been the worst thing he'd ever had to deal with, though. The shock of seeing his dead wife had been terrible enough. To be told she hadn't been alone in her bed had been an additional blow he hadn't been able to handle.

The police had been so understanding. Apologetic, really, at having to deliver the extra blow. Sympathetic. It could be kept quiet, if that's what he would prefer.

Of course he would. Nobody would ever know. Emma certainly didn't need to know, even though it was tempting to tell her, thanks to the look of appalled empathy in her eyes. Did he want her to really understand? To feel... sorry for him?

No.

He cleared his throat. 'She'd died from the smoke inhalation, not the flames.'

Flames. How shocking had it been to see that paper chain erupt? The children must have been terrified and it was all because he hadn't known what to do with that dreadful surge of feelings that had been unbearable.

'It was very late by the time I got back. My mother was asleep upstairs with the children and it was the early hours of Christmas Day. The day I would have to tell my bairns that their mummy wasn't coming home.'

'I'm so sorry, Adam.' The words were a whisper and when he looked up again there were tears rolling down the side of Emma's nose.

'It's not your fault.' He wanted to reach out and catch one of those tears with his thumb and wipe it away. He wanted to go upstairs and kiss his children and tell them he was sorry and that they would never see him like that again. He would do that. Soon. Even if they were asleep. And then he'd do it again tomorrow.

'None of this is your fault,' he told Emma. 'It's me.'

'It's me who's tried to force you to bring Christmas into the house. I'm so sorry. For your loss and for the hurt I've caused. I was thinking about the children and *their* Christmas and I lost sight of how much it might hurt you.'

Emma was clearly not a practised whisky drinker. She took a gulp that made her cough and splutter and Adam had to resist the urge to pat her on the back.

To smile even.

'I'll get rid of everything,' she offered. 'I'll explain to the children that you're not ready to celebrate Christmas yet. That we can go and see the tree in the village and we don't need to have one in the house. We can take the paper chains to school and I'm sure Caitlin will let us put them up in the classroom. And I'll—'

Adam reached out and put his hand over hers. Only because she wasn't looking at him and he wanted her to stop talking.

It worked. Emma went very still but Adam didn't take his hand away from hers. It felt tiny and soft and warm under his and he liked it.

'No,' he said softly. 'What you can do is show me how to make a paper chain. I want to fix this one so it's right for when the children come down in the morning. And tomorrow I'll go up into the attic and find the box of decorations for the tree.'

'Oh...' There was a sparkle in those blue-grey eyes that looked like more than the remnants of tears. And her hand moved under his. Turned and twisted so that her fingers were grasping his palm. *Squeezing* it. 'Really? You'll let us have a real Christmas? In the *house*?'

'Aye.' It was impossible not to catch a little bit of that childlike enthusiasm. The sheer joy that was breaking through. 'Three years of grief is enough, I'm thinking. We'll do this for the children.'

'Oh...' Emma jumped to her feet and Adam found himself standing up, too. Had he guessed that she would stand on tiptoe and throw her arms around him?

'*Thank* you, Adam. Thank you *so* much...'

'I'll talk to the hall committee too, about Jemima being in the play. I still think it's a bit daft but if they know it's for the children—for the first real Christmas they're going to celebrate since their mother died—they might just come on board.'

She was beaming up at him. Impossible not to smile back. She was so loving, this gypsy waif of a woman. So full of joy.

It was he who should be thanking her. He knew that but somehow the words wouldn't form themselves. Instead, he felt his arms go around her. How long had it been since he'd felt the soft curves of a woman like this?

Three years—that's how long. He'd actually forgotten how *good* it could feel.

He smiled back at her and she stretched up even more and kissed him on the cheek. Except that he moved his head somehow and it was the corner of his mouth that her lips brushed.

And, heaven help him, for a heartbeat he wanted her to do it again. To kiss him.

And not on his cheek.

Maybe Emma had sensed the longing. She sprang away from him. 'I'll get the sticky paper,' she said. 'There's plenty left.'

Oh...*help*...

She hadn't intended to kiss Adam at all and she *certainly* hadn't been aiming anywhere near his mouth, but he'd moved somehow and her lips had been aware of exactly where they'd landed, albeit so briefly.

She'd dismissed the tingle that had run right through her body as embarrassment but it wasn't going away as they sat cutting strips of coloured paper. It was more than embarrassment at being so inappropriate, wasn't it? And hadn't the lines between employer and employee been blurred beyond recognition by Adam talking about something so personal?

So incredibly *sad*…

Emma could understand completely how Adam felt about celebrating Christmas now and yet he was prepared to put his own feelings aside for the sake of the children.

How brave was that?

She stole a glance at the man sitting at the table with her. Such a serious face. And skilful hands that could probably do all sorts of incredibly intricate medical procedures but were currently being used with intense concentration to manipulate strips of rainbow-coloured paper. It was ridiculous but she actually felt…*proud* of Adam? For putting his children first. For being staunch.

And that seemed to intensify the lingering tingle. Emma needed to distract herself before she said or did something else that might overstep a boundary that was becoming more difficult to identify. She looked at what Adam was doing. He had made two loops. Separate loops.

'Once you've made one loop, you need to thread the next strip through before you stick it into a loop. That's how they join up. Like this…see?'

'Oh…aye…' Adam made a face. 'I was distracted by the taste. I might need another wee dram to wash it away soon.'

He looked happier when he had three and then four loops joined together. 'I can see why the children enjoyed doing this. It's quite satisfying, isn't it?'

Emma nodded, smiling as she remembered how much

the twins had loved the activity. 'Poppy and Ollie are easy to entertain,' she told him. 'They're gorgeous children.'

'You manage them very well. For someone who's never been a nanny, you're doing a good job, Emma.'

It felt like high praise. Especially when it came with a smile and a softening of those dark eyes. Yes...the lines of those boundaries had definitely been blurred. Where exactly did they stop now?

Inexplicably, that silent query kicked the tingle up by several notches. In a kind of backwards trickle that went through her limbs and pooled somewhere deep inside.

'How do you know how to get on so well with kids? You said you didn't have any younger brothers or sisters, didn't you?'

She nodded again. 'I did have a kind of older brother, though. Jack.'

'A kind of brother?'

'He was the son of my parents' best friends. A lot older than me but we got on really well. Still do. He's... important in my life.'

That was an understatement but Adam had obviously picked up on the vibe.

'Your boyfriend?'

'Heavens, no...' Emma almost smiled at the question but there was something in Adam's tone that she couldn't place. Did he *want* her to have a boyfriend? So that those boundaries were clearly flagged? What would happen when he knew the truth?

'I love Jack dearly,' she said quietly, 'but definitely in the brother category. And he's happily married now with his first baby on the way. No...he's even more special now because he became a doctor and then a specialist in oncology. He kept Mum going for a lot longer than she might have had otherwise and she had a good quality of life until…the end.'

And he'd been her primary physician ever since her own diagnosis. How many people were lucky enough to get a doctor who cared so much? Who was so determined to succeed?

'How long ago did you lose your mother?'

'Just last year.' Emma met his sympathetic gaze. The boundary lines were totally invisible now. It felt like she was sitting here talking to a friend, not her employer. 'And I miss her terribly. You're very lucky to have your mum as part of your life.'

'I know. But she does too much. It's not fair…' For a heartbeat, as Adam held her gaze, it seemed like he was going to say something else. About his mother? About *her*?

Something that might reveal he was feeling the extraordinary connection that had Emma slightly stunned?

No. Emma couldn't tell if it was relief or disappointment that coursed through her as Adam frowned and looked away. Normal service was being resumed. Maybe a breathing space was a good idea. For both of them. Or maybe she'd just been imagining that connection.

He held up his paper chain.

'Will this be long enough, do you think? When it's joined to yours?'

By the time breakfast was ready the next day, the paper chains were back in place as though nothing had happened last night.

Poppy and Oliver had bounced back to normal in the delightful way children could. Not only was Adam apparently forgiven for his outburst, the twins were impressed that he had fixed the paper chain himself.

'All by yourself?' Poppy asked.

'Emma showed me what to do.'

Emma looked up from where she was spooning porridge into bowls and grinned at him. 'I expect you could have worked it out all by yourself,' she said generously. 'Coffee?'

'Please.' It made him feel good to remember their time together last night. Talking about things he would never normally share. Feeling as if he was in the company of someone he could talk to about anything at all. Adam began to smile back at her but he was aware of the intense scrutiny of the children so he smiled at them instead.

'It makes your mouth taste funny after a while, doesn't it? Licking the sticky paper?'

'Aye...' Oliver nodded solemnly as he climbed onto his chair. 'It does at that.'

Adam's mouth twitched into a wider smile at the adult turn of phrase from his small son but then it faded as he caught the glance slanted in his direction as Oliver reached for his glass of milk. There was a hint of wariness in those brown eyes that were so like his own. Ollie was on his best behaviour, wasn't he? Just in case...

And that hurt. How often had his children tiptoed around him? he wondered. To stop him being cross.

Or sad.

The resolution to put the years of mourning behind this family and move forward had seemed more of a mountain to climb when he'd woken this morning after a somewhat disturbing dream that had included the new nanny but Adam had gathered it back and shored it up.

Things *were* going to change around here.

And Christmas was the perfect time to start.

'Tonight,' he told his children, 'when I get home from work, we're going to have an expedition.'

'What's an exposition?' Poppy looked at the bowl Emma put in front of her. 'I don't like porridge.' She frowned. 'It's *icky*.'

'Not when you put a little bit of cream and some brown sugar on it. Here, I'll help you.'

'An expedition is an adventure,' Adam told his daughter. 'And when I get home, we'll get the ladder out and go up into the attic.'

Oliver stopped making roads through his porridge with his spoon. 'The *attic*? Where the ghost is?'

'There's no such thing as ghosts,' Adam said firmly. 'It's where the box of Christmas decorations is. We're going to find it and then decorate your tree.'

Poppy's gasp was one of pure excitement. She had to climb off her chair, onto her father's lap, throw her arms around his neck and plant a kiss—sticky with brown sugar—in the middle of his cheek.

The dogs caught the excitement. Benji barked and chased his tail over by the fire and staid old Bob's tail was waving like a flag. Even studious little Oliver was grinning widely.

Adam could almost taste the sweetness of the sugary kiss Poppy had bestowed but when she returned to her own chair he looked across to where Emma was sitting with her own bowl of porridge. He might have expected to see her beaming at him with that infectious joy she had but, instead, her smile was poignant and there was a sparkle in her eyes that reminded him of when they had been full of tears.

She knew how much of an effort he was making here. That things were going to change and that this was going to be the best Christmas he could manage for the twins.

The memory of that butterfly's-wing touch of Emma's lips on the corner of his mouth came flooding back. And that peculiar moment when he'd caught her gaze after she talked about her mother and he'd had the disconcerting notion that he was actually falling into those blue pools. And that merged into a remnant of his dream that he couldn't quite catch and probably didn't want to anyway, but *something* was hanging in the air between him and Emma.

Yes. Things were changing. Had he thrown a pebble into a still pond and the ripples were only just beginning?

That was disturbing. Adam fed his crust to the dogs and drained the last of his coffee.

'Time for me to go to work,' he announced gruffly, careful to avoid any more eye contact with Emma that might add to the alarming impression that he might have started something that could get completely out of control.

'You won't forget, will you, Dad?'

'What's that, Ollie?'

'About the adventure. In the attic.'

'No, son.' He ruffled Oliver's hair. 'I won't forget. I promise.'

He kissed Poppy and nodded farewell to Emma. And it only took that microsecond of a look to realise that there were other things he wasn't about to forget either.

However much he wished he could.

CHAPTER SIX

HE'D BEEN WRONG about the ghost in the attic.

Adam realised that the instant he stepped through the hole in the ceiling, even before he turned to help first Oliver and then Poppy to climb off the steep set of stairs cleverly concealed behind a door that had been locked for years.

The light switch he flicked made several bulbs glow but the light was inadequate for the huge space. Despite the shadows, however, his gaze went straight towards that long rack of dresses in the far corner where the roofline sloped sharply towards the small latticed windows. And the stacks of boxes beside it, full of other clothing and shoes and handbags. He could even make out the jewellery case sitting on top.

They represented what had attracted him to Tania in the first place. The beauty. The glamour. In retrospect he was ashamed of how shallow it was to judge people on their outward appearance like that. Look at how he'd judged Emma in her oversized clothes with her musical accessory as a refugee from the sixties. If fate hadn't stepped in and made it imperative that he give her a chance, he might never have discovered what an astonishing person lay beneath that appearance.

And fate had been responsible for discovering the real

reason for more and more of those 'shopping' trips that Tania had needed to keep her happy. Had she even worn half those clothes or had they only ever been a mask for her infidelity?

The presence of Tania's ghost was all he was aware of by the time Emma's head appeared through the hole.

'Oof… I feel like I'm climbing a mountain.'

The steps were certainly steep but shouldn't have been enough to make a young woman like Emma seem out of breath. Adam could feel his frown deepening as he automatically held out his hand to assist her. For a moment he thought she might refuse the offer but then he felt his hand grasped firmly as she climbed the last of the steps.

Like the children, Emma's eyes widened as she looked around. 'Oh, *wow*… This is a *real* attic. Full of *treasure*.'

She was grinning at Adam now and she still hadn't let go of his hand. He could feel the connection and it was warm and as alive as the sparkle in her eyes.

She'd never be able to cover up a lie, would she? Not with the way her emotions played over her face like this. The idea that she might need to lie felt ridiculous. The conviction that Emma would never be unfaithful to a man she loved came from nowhere.

So did the unexpected pang of something that felt like envy. Letting go of her hand didn't entirely dispel the disturbing sensation. Whoever it was, he would be a very lucky man.

'Ohh…' The gasp from Poppy was full of wonder. 'Look, Emma… It's a *pram*.'

She ran towards the part of the attic on the opposite side from where Tania's effects had been stored. Alongside an antique pram that had probably carried his grandmother and the double model that had been for the twins much more recently, was a smaller cane one. The one that had caught Poppy's eye had been made for small girls to carry dolls in. Adam had completely forgotten it was up here.

'Can I play with it, Daddy? *Please*?'

'Of course you can, chicken. We'll take it downstairs and clean all the dust off. I think it might have been Gran's when she was a little girl like you.'

Maybe it was the delight on Poppy's face or the warmth he could still feel from Emma's hand but the presence of Tania's ghost was receding. Being pushed into the past where it belonged by not only being in the present but thinking about the immediate future when they would all be safely downstairs and he could lock the old door again.

Poppy was squeaking with pleasure as she manoeuvred the cane pram out from behind the bigger wheels of the others. Oliver was not far away from her, peering into a tin trunk in front of a pile of old leather suitcases. His quietness wasn't unusual but the intent body language was unmistakeable.

'What have you found, Ollie?'

'I think it's a...*train*.'

It had been some time since he'd let go of Emma's hand. Odd that he still could feel the absence of it so strongly. Maybe moving further away from her would help. Adam walked towards his son.

'It *is* a train. An old wind-up one.' He lifted the heavy, metal engine from the trunk to hand to Oliver and then reached to pick up something else. 'These are the tracks that you can clip together. I used to play with it when I was your age, Ollie. And my father played with it when *he* was a little boy. I'm pretty sure he got it for a Christmas present one year.'

Oliver's face was solemn. 'That's what I'd like for *my* Christmas present.'

'You can't buy these now.' Emma had come over to look as well. 'They're very old and very special. Antiques. Adam, this is extraordinary. Is that a *harp* over there?'

'Aye.' There was a dusty, old cello keeping it company. Music had been in his family for generations. When had it stopped so completely? When his desire to make it had died along with the trauma of Tania's death?

Oliver was crouching beside the tin trunk with the train engine cradled in his arms.

Adam crouched down beside him. 'You don't have to wait till Christmas, Ollie. We'll take this downstairs, too, and you can play with it whenever you want.'

Oliver looked as though he couldn't believe his luck. As if something truly magic had just happened, and something squeezed inside Adam's chest. How easy it was to make children happy but he had never given a thought to the abandoned toys up here. He would never have thought of even unlocking that door if he hadn't remembered the Christmas decorations.

And he wouldn't have considered retrieving those if it hadn't been for Emma pushing him towards celebrating Christmas again.

Right now Emma was plucking the strings of the old harp, sending dust motes flying into the dim light in the attic. And she was singing…just softly. More of a hum really—as though she was in her own world and making music came as naturally as breathing.

Poppy had left the cane pram. She had a sad old teddy bear with an almost severed arm dangling from one hand and she was skipping through the gaps towards *that* corner.

Adam got to his feet hurriedly. 'Let's find those decorations,' he said. 'And get downstairs. I can hear Benji
crying in the kitchen.'

But it was too late. Poppy had found the rack of
dresses and her cry of delight made Emma stop playing
with the harp and look up. Adam tried to distract them.
He'd had an idea of where the boxes of decorations were
and he flipped one open and held up a handful of tinsel
and then a huge silver star.

'Here we are. Look at this star. Shall we put it on top
of our tree?'

'Daddy…are these *Mummy's* dresses?'

The shocked look on Emma's face said it all. The ghost
was here again. The tug of nostalgia and the pleasure in
finding unexpected gifts for his children vanished. Now
he could feel the pain of loss yet again. The *guilt*. The
burden of the lie that kept the mother of his children as
a perfect memory.

'It's a *blue* dress. Emma, look. You're going to make
me a blue dress for when I'm Mary in the play, aren't
you?'

'Um…yeah…' Emma had started to go towards Poppy
but she'd stopped right beside Adam and she gave him
an uncertain glance. 'Come on, sweetheart. We need to
go downstairs. It's nearly teatime.'

But Poppy wouldn't let go of the folds of the shimmery,
blue dress. 'Why are Mummy's clothes here, Daddy?'

Adam had to clear his throat. 'I…' What could he say?
He'd had to get them out of sight and this had seemed
the quickest and easiest solution? 'Maybe I thought you'd
want them one day, Poppy.'

He hoped she wouldn't, he realised suddenly. He
didn't want his daughter growing up to be consumed
with keeping up appearances. Better that she didn't care.

That she was happy to wear baggy jumpers and peculiar, bright hats and could shine with an inner joy instead. Like Emma.

'I want this one *now*, Daddy. For the play.'

'It wouldn't fit you.'

'Emma could make it fit.'

'Could you?' Adam caught Emma's gaze again.

She still looked uncertain but nodded. 'I guess so… but…'

'That's settled, then.' Adam wanted to get out of there. As quickly as possible. 'You and Ollie go downstairs with Emma and I'll bring the dress down with the other things.'

Emma helped the children down the steps but then her head appeared again.

'You don't have to do this,' she said quietly. 'I can explain to Poppy. We can find some fabric to make her dress.'

'They're only clothes,' Adam growled. He shoved the rolled-up dress towards her. 'This one was never even worn—it's still got its label on it. They're only *clothes*,' he repeated, turning away to pick up a box. 'I should never have kept them.'

But Emma was still there when he went to put the box down close to the steps. 'You can still change your mind later.'

'I won't.'

'You might.' There was a curve to Emma's lips that suggested sympathy but she wasn't looking at his face. She was staring at the hand he had curled around the corner of the box of decorations. His left hand.

The one that still carried his wedding ring.

And then Emma was gone and he heard Poppy's excited voice fading as she went along the hallway, telling

Emma that she wanted the dress to be really long so that it floated on the ground.

It took time to get the treasures down the steps, especially when he had to unpack half the tin trunk because it was so heavy. Even in the inadequate light every movement seemed to create a glint on that gold band around his finger—an accessory he never normally noticed at all.

Why *was* he still wearing his wedding ring? Because everybody assumed that he kept it on as a tribute to a perfect marriage and they would have noticed the moment he'd removed it? A perfect marriage? Good grief... In the short time Emma had been here, it felt like she'd been more of a mother to his children than Tania had been. Guilt nipped on the heels of that admission. It wasn't something he'd ever needed to acknowledge—not when his mother had always been there to fill in the gaps that his nannies couldn't.

Or did he still wear the ring because he wanted to punish himself? To keep a permanent reminder of his failure as a husband in clear view?

It was, after all, *his* fault that his children were growing up without their mother, wasn't it? Had he been too absorbed in his work or too besotted with his babies to give Tania what she needed?

The ring had served its purpose even if he'd never articulated what that was. There had been times when the truth had been like acid, eating away at him, and he'd been desperate to tell someone. His mother or his sister perhaps. And then he'd touch the back of the ring with his thumb and would know that he couldn't.

Even the remote possibility that his children could learn the truth about their mother and be hurt by it was enough. This was a burden he had to carry alone. For ever.

He might have been wrong about there being no ghost in the attic but he'd been right when he'd worried about the ripple effect of things changing.

Unusually, he could actually *feel* that ring on his finger, without touching it with his thumb, late that night as he climbed the stairs to go to bed. They hadn't ended up decorating the tree after dinner because he'd spent the time before the children went to bed setting up the clockwork train set for Oliver, and Emma had been busy helping Poppy clean the cane pram. And when they'd looked into the box the children had been a little disappointed by the ornaments.

'They're all the same colour,' Poppy had pointed out. 'They're all *silver*.'

Of course they were. Everything Tania had done could have been photographed for a home and garden magazine, including the silver perfection of the family Christmas tree.

'I could get some special paint,' Emma had offered. 'And we could make them all sorts of colours…if that's all right with Daddy.'

Of course it was all right. How did she always seem to find an answer to everything that would make things better?

Would she have an answer to what he should do about the ring that seemed to be strangling his finger?

He could hear the soft sound of her singing again and, as had become a habit, he stopped before turning towards the other hallway and listened for a minute. The song was becoming hauntingly familiar, even though he was sure he'd never heard it before Emma had come into the house.

Was she sitting on her bed, with her guitar cradled on her lap and her head bent as she sang quietly? Did she have the fire going perhaps, with the light of the flames bringing out the flecks of red-gold he'd noticed in her hair sometimes?

The urge to find out was powerful. He could find an excuse to tap on her door, couldn't he? To reassure her that the blue dress meant nothing perhaps, and that she was more than welcome to cut it up to make Poppy's costume?

Any excuse would do, if it meant he could be close to her for an extra minute or two.

Because he was starting to feel lonely when he wasn't?

With a mental shake Adam stepped firmly towards his own room. She wasn't the first nanny his children had had and she probably wouldn't be the last. It was just as well this was a temporary position, though, because he'd never felt this way about any of the women who'd come to live here and look after his children before.

About any women he'd met in the last few years, come to that.

Maybe it was part of the ripple effect. The step forward. Something had been unlocked when he'd agreed that three years of grief was more than enough. Perhaps his body was following his heart and finally waking up again.

Three years of being celibate wasn't natural for anyone. It didn't mean that he had to fall for someone who happened to be in the near vicinity. It didn't mean he had to fall for anyone.

No. The last time that had happened had ended up almost ruining his life. He wasn't going to let it happen again.

Ever.

The solution, Adam decided over the next few days, was to focus on his work.

His priority in life was his children, of course, but

work came a close second. It had been his father, the first
Dr McAllister, who'd built up this small general practice.
Without it, the villagers would have to travel fifteen miles
or so to the nearest town and a lot of them would find
that difficult enough to make their health care precari-
ous, especially in the middle of a harsh Scottish winter.

People like old Mrs Robertson, who needed dressings
changed on her diabetic ulcers every couple of days and
was on the list for this afternoon's house calls. And Joan
McClintock, who had a phobia about getting into any ve-
hicles smaller than a bus and was only happy when things
were within walking distance. She was in the waiting
room again this morning, as his somewhat disconcerting working week drew to a close.

At least here Adam could stop thinking about the
Christmas tree in his living room sporting a rainbow
of brightly painted balls that had only been the starting
point for the hand-made decorations that Emma seemed
to have unlimited inspiration about. Like the gingerbread
stars she had baked last night and the children had helped
to decorate with brightly coloured sweets.

It was probably just as well that the gingerbread was
destined to be only decorative if Emma's baking skills
were on a par with her cooking. The meals this week had
been a fair step down from what his mother had left in
the freezer. Not that the children had complained about
the rather burnt sausages and that peculiar shepherd's
pie. Everything Emma did was wonderful in Poppy's
eyes and Oliver wasn't allowed to go and play with the
clockwork train until he'd finished his dinner so even
the carrots were disappearing in record time these days.

Adam found himself smiling as he walked through
the waiting room. Miss McClintock looked surprised but
nodded back at him. Old Jock, who was sitting in the cor-

ner, disappeared further under the brim of his cap. The smile faded. Old Jock—the farmer who owned the land behind his where the skating pond was located—was as tough as old boots. What was he doing in here, waiting to see the doctor?

And had he really thought that work was the solution to forgetting about the ripples disrupting his personal life?

It didn't help that Caitlin McMurray, the schoolteacher, came rushing in with a wailing small child even before he could call Joan McClintock into the consulting room.

'It's Ben,' she said. 'He jammed his finger in the art cupboard.'

'Come straight in,' Adam told her. 'Eileen, could you call Ben's mother, please, and get her to come in?'

'I can stay with him for a bit.' Caitlin had to raise her voice over the crying. 'Emma's practising carols with the children and the senior teacher's keeping an eye on everything.'

Adam eyed the handkerchief tied around Ben's finger. There was blood seeping through the makeshift dressing.

'Let's have a look at this finger, young man.'

'No-o-o… It's going to hurt.'

Distraction was needed. 'Did our Oliver tell you about the train he found in our attic?'

'Aye…but we didn't believe him.' Ben sniffed loudly. 'He said it's got a tunnel and a bridge even.'

'Well, it's true. It's a bonny wee train. I played with it when I was a wee boy, too.' Adam had the finger exposed now. A bit squashed but there were no bones broken. The pain was coming from the blood accumulating under the nail and that could be swiftly fixed with a heated needle.

'And he says he's bringing a donkey to the Christmas play.'

Adam raised his gaze to Caitlin's. 'Did the committee agree, then?'

'Aye. And that's not all. Have you heard about the recording?'

'What recording?'

'Moira Findlay heard about the children singing the carols and she came to listen. She says that Emma's got the voice of an angel and she's ne'er heard small children singing sae well. That's when we got the *idea.*'

'Oh?' Adam struck a match to get the end of a sterile needle hot enough. Ben was watching suspiciously.

'We're going to make a CD of the carols. To sell and raise funds to help fix the village hall. Or get a new piano for the school. Maybe both. She's amazing, isn't she, Dr McAllister?'

'It does sound like a grand idea. Moira's a clever woman.'

'Not Moira…' Caitlin laughed. 'I mean Emma. How lucky are we that she came to be the twins' nanny?'

'Look at that, Ben… Out the window… Was that a… *reindeer*?'

The split second it took for Ben to realise he'd been duped was enough to get near his nail with the needle and release the pressure. A single, outraged wail and then Ben stared at his finger and blinked in surprise.

'Not so sore now?' Adam swabbed it gently with some disinfectant. 'We'll put a nice big bandage on it and you can get back to singing your carols.'

With Emma.

'I hear she sings like an angel,' Joan McClintock informed him minutes later. 'Eileen says she might be joining the choir.'

'I don't know that she'll have time for that,' Adam

said. 'And she's only here until my mother gets back from Canada.'

'Och, well…we'll see about that, then, won't we?' The nod was knowing.

'Aye. We will.' Adam reached for the blood-pressure cuff. 'Now, let's see if that blood pressure's come down a wee bit. Are you still getting the giddy spells?'

Even Old Jock had something to say about Emma when it came to his turn.

'I'm losing my puff,' he told Adam. 'And it's no' helping with the pipes. Yon lassie o' yours saw me sittin' down after I was playin' in by the tree, like I always do at Christmastime. She tol' me to come and see you.'

'I'll have a listen to your chest,' Adam said. 'Your dad had problems with his heart, didn't he? We might do a test on that, too.'

'Aye.' Jock took his cap off. 'You do what you need to, lad. That lassie said you'd find out what was ailin' me.'

How could a complete stranger weave herself into the lives of other people so quickly? It seemed like the whole village was being touched by Emma's arrival in Braeburn. Maybe she didn't have a gypsy streak after all, because the sort of magic she was creating was more like that of a fairy.

A Christmas fairy.

And magic wasn't the only thing she was weaving. On Saturday afternoon, when it had stopped raining, they had taken Jemima down into the orchard so that Oliver could practise leading her, with Poppy riding. Not only had their little donkey proved herself very co-operative, Emma had spotted the greenery amongst the bare branches of an old apple tree.

'Is that mistletoe? *Real* mistletoe?'

'Aye. Looks like it.'

'Can we pick it?' Emma had asked. 'For Christmas?'

'It's poisonous,' Adam had told her. 'Causes gastro-intestinal and cardiovascular problems.'

'We won't *eat* it, silly.' Emma had laughed. 'I'm going to make a wreath.'

So here she was, sitting at the kitchen table under all the paper chains, after the children were in bed, cutting sprigs of the mistletoe and weaving them around a circle she'd made with some wire she'd unearthed out in the barn. Adam had poured himself a wee dram to finish the day with and he paused to watch what she was doing.

'Where did it come from?' she asked. 'Do you know? The tradition of kissing under the mistletoe, that is.'

Kissing…

Adam stared down at Emma's deft hands weaving the sprigs into place. And at the back of her head, where the light was creating those copper glints in her curls. He took a mouthful of his whisky.

'It's very old,' he said. 'I've heard that it got hung somewhere and the young men had the privilege of kiss-ing the girls underneath it, but every time they did they had to pick one of the berries, and when the berries had all been picked, the privilege ceased.'

Emma held up the half-finished wreath with its clus-ters of waxy white berries. 'It's got a lot of them,' she said, tilting her head to smile up at Adam.

That did it. The magic was too strong to resist. Adam put his glass down and then reached out and plucked one of the tiny berries from the wreath.

Emma's eyes widened. 'You can't do that,' she ob-jected. 'You haven't kissed a girl.'

Adam didn't say anything. He just leaned down until there was no mistaking his intention.

And Emma didn't turn her face away. If anything, she tilted her chin so that her lips parted, and for a heart-beat—and then two—she held his gaze.

There was surprise in those blue eyes. She hadn't expected this but, then, neither had Adam. And she could feel the magic, too—he was sure of that, because there was a kind of wonder in her eyes as well.

Joy was always lurking there, he suspected, but this was an invitation to share it. An invitation no man could resist.

The moment his lips touched Emma's, the tiny white berry fell from his fingers and rolled somewhere under the table. Adam wasn't aware of dropping it. He was aware of nothing but the softness of Emma's lips and the silky feel of her curls as he cupped her head in his hand. And then he was aware of a desire for more than this kiss. A fierce shaft of desire that came from nowhere and with more force than he'd ever felt in his life.

He had to break the contact. Step back. Wonder how on earth he was going to deal with what had just happened when his senses were still reeling.

Emma's eyes were closed. He liked it that she'd closed her eyes. And then she sighed happily and smiled. There was no embarrassment in her eyes when she opened them. No expectation that any explanation or apology was needed.

'There you go,' she said softly. 'That's where it came from, I guess. Mistletoe is magical. I'd better finish this and hang it somewhere safe.'

'Aye.' Adam drained the rest of his whisky and took the glass to the sink.

What did she mean by 'safe'? Somewhere he couldn't find it or somewhere he *could*?

He hoped she wanted to put it somewhere he could find it.

There were a lot of berries left on those twigs.

CHAPTER SEVEN

FOR THE FIRST time in her life Emma Sinclair understood why they called it 'falling' in love.

Because she could feel that her balance was teetering. That there was a chasm very nearby that she couldn't afford to fall into. She could get hurt.

Or hurt someone else.

Poppy and Oliver perhaps?

Or Adam?

Her hands stilled in their task of hemming, sinking to end up in the folds of the silky blue dress puddled in her lap, as she stared through the window. It was snowing, she realised with a childish bubble of excitement.

And then she remembered the kiss yet again and the bubble exploded into something decidedly more adult and compelling.

Desire—pure and simple.

Except it wasn't that simple, was it? Oh, she'd noticed how good looking Adam McAllister was in the first moments of meeting him but she'd been a little afraid of him, too, if she was honest. The fierceness of him. The gruffness that came across as anger. The hidden depths that she'd glimpsed on that awful night when he'd ripped down the paper chains and caused the fire. And now she could add the capacity for passion into what this man was keeping hidden because she'd felt it in the touch of his lips.

She'd glimpsed the softer side to him as well, in the love he had for his children and the bond he had with his dogs. Pulling her gaze away from the softly drifting snowflakes, Emma glanced towards the fire. Benji lay on his back like a puppy, his speckled belly exposed, but Bob had his nose on his paws and he was watching Emma. She could swear that the old dog knew exactly what she was thinking and that the liquid gaze was encouraging.

He's worth loving, it seemed to say. *You won't be sorry.*

'But I can't, Bob.' Emma actually spoke aloud. 'I'm only here for a little bit longer.'

Time didn't matter to dogs, though, did it? They took their joy as it appeared, with no questions asked. Even if they were old or sick, they could still be in the moment and experience that joy a hundred per cent.

People could learn a lot from dogs. Especially people who could be facing a terminal illness?

What if she let herself fall for Adam—even if it was only for a blink in time? It wasn't just for the small McAllister family that she'd resolved to make this the best-ever Christmas for, was it?

If it was going to be *her* last Christmas, shouldn't she make it the best ever one for herself, too?

'It's been *such* a long time, Bob,' she whispered.

Such a long time since she had been loved...

Dear Lord, but it was tempting.

Bob's ears were pricked now. He looked like he was asking her a question and Emma found herself smiling at the dog. No—she didn't *have* to disappear right after Christmas, when Catherine McAllister returned, did she? Adam was still going to need a nanny and it wasn't as if she had another job prospect lined up. She didn't need to work at all, in actual fact, because the small inheritance from her mother would be enough for quite some time.

But she couldn't offer Adam anything real. She didn't do that kind of commitment. How could she, when she couldn't offer any guarantee of permanence? When, instead, she could be sentencing someone to share things no one would choose to share.

And he wouldn't want it anyway, would he? The blue of the fabric in her lap seemed to glow more brightly. How could anyone compete with the ghost of the perfect wife and mother? The love of his life that had been tragically ripped away from him and their beloved children?

The recently changed ring tone on her phone was for Christmas and Bob got to his feet as 'Jingle Bells' began. It was getting louder by the time Emma found the phone beneath the shimmery blue fabric.

'It'll be Sharon, I expect,' she said, as Bob gave her hand a helpful nudge.

Except it wasn't.

'*Jack…*' It was such a surprise to hear from him. A shock even, because it pulled her back instantly to somewhere she'd managed to distract herself from completely in the last couple of weeks.

'Hey, Emma. How's it going up there in the wilds of Scotland?'

'It's snowing,' she told him happily. 'And it's just gorgeous. What's it like in London?'

'Cold and grey. No snow. That's why I thought I'd pop up for a visit next week.'

'What?' Emma blinked. The relationship was a complicated mix sometimes and she wasn't sure if he was wearing his 'close friend' or 'oncologist' hat right now. '*Why?*'

'I'm meeting with an oncology guru who happens to

be over from the States, tracing his family tree. I must have told you about that international research project we're both involved in. Jenny says I bore everyone with it.' He chuckled, unrepentant. 'Anyway, I said I'd fly up for the day and then I had this idea and got hold of a mate who works in the infirmary in Edinburgh. I pulled a few strings but...how would you feel about having your BMT and maybe getting the results by Christmas?'

'Oh...' Emma had to swallow hard. The unpleasant prospect of having a bone-marrow aspiration done for testing had been off her agenda until she got back to London. 'I'm...not sure how I feel about that, Jack. I...' Oh, help. She could hear the wobble in her voice that threatened tears. 'I was trying to forget about it, you know? To make this Christmas really special, in case...in case...'

'I know.' There was a short silence and then Jack's voice was gentle. 'Things are going to shut down for a while down here, what with Christmas and then New Year. And the baby's not far off making an appearance, which could complicate things a bit for me, but it's entirely your call. It was just an idea.'

Another silence as Emma's mind raced. She would be thinking about it again now, wouldn't she? Distraction would get harder. It could spoil things.

She heard Jack clear his throat. 'How 'bout this for another idea? Get the test done and, if the result comes through in time and it's what we hope it's going to be, I can give it to you as your Christmas present. And we can all really celebrate.'

He was including Sharon in that 'we'. They'd got on famously from the moment they'd first met and had worked closely together to get Emma through the toughest of times.

'And if it isn't?' Emma's voice was so soft she didn't think Jack would hear her but he did.

'Then we'll deal with it. After Christmas.'

Emma closed her eyes. That errant thought that she could perhaps stay in Braeburn longer than originally intended was still lurking in the back of her head and it would be much more convenient to pop over to Edinburgh for the test than go all the way back to London. And the result of that test couldn't possibly be devastating, could it, given that she was feeling so good at the moment? The physical exhaustion that used to ambush her all the time had virtually disappeared so she knew she was getting stronger every day. How amazing would it be to get confirmation of something so wonderful as a Christmas gift?

'Okay...Let me find a pen and paper and I'll take down the details.'

It was proving to be a long day for Adam. Another one where it was difficult to separate his professional and personal lives.

He couldn't blame his patients for making Emma's presence felt in his consulting room or when he was making his house calls, though. No...it was his own disobedient mind.

Or maybe he should blame his body.

He hadn't touched a woman in that way since his wife had died. Hadn't even thought of touching like that, let alone *kissing* someone.

And it wouldn't go away. The memory of how soft her lips had been. How sweet the taste of her had been. The shaft of desire for more that had been sharp enough to be both a physical and emotional pain.

Maybe that was what was making his mouth go a little dry at intervals today and increasing his heart rate until he could feel it thumping against his ribs. Too much adrenaline being produced. And why?

He knew if he looked a little more closely, he would know exactly why.

Fear.

Fear of being inadequate.

What man wouldn't have lost confidence? Especially when avoidance had been the defence method of choice and it was now ingrained as a way of life? His children, his work and his community. Those were the things he could do and do well. Being a husband or even a lover?

That was what he wasn't so sure of any more.

He'd always been good at avoidance, too. Even way back he'd made allowances for Tania's dissatisfaction. She was a city girl, born and bred, so of course she found a small village like Braeburn boring to the point of suffocation.

Emma was a city girl, too, wasn't she? She seemed to love village life but it was just a change for her. A very temporary change. Maybe the novelty would wear off.

Adam drove back to the medical centre that afternoon after visiting a sick baby on a farm that lay on the very outskirts of his practice area. It was starting to snow lightly and the stone walls and hedgerows looked like they were being dusted with icing sugar. The fairy-lights on the village shops were twinkling merrily and the tree in the square couldn't have looked any more perfect.

He could see Old Jock over by the pub with his bagpipes under his arm. Hopefully, he'd go in by the fire and have a wee dram instead of getting too cold, serenading the village. He'd have to chase up those test results when he got back to his office. Something was going on with Jock and while nothing obvious had been noticeable when he'd examined the older man the other day, Adam wasn't happy about it.

He cared deeply about the people of Braeburn. *His* people. It wasn't just the physical beauty of this place that made it paradise for those who could see it. It was the embrace of a community tight enough to seem like an extended family with both its positive—supportive— side and the more negative—intrusive—one.

Eileen was in position, as always, guarding the reception desk, when he got back to the medical centre.

'Any calls while I've been out?'

'No' yet.' Eileen clicked her tongue. 'There will be, mind... It's snowing.'

'Aye.'

'Someone will fall over and break something, you mark my words.'

Adam smiled and Eileen looked shocked.

'It's no laughin' matter, Dr McAllister.'

'No.'

But the smile still lingered as he went into his office to make some calls. He needed to chase up Old Jock's results and ring to see how the Jessops' premature baby was doing. Still touch and go as far as he knew, but at least the little scrap was hanging in there.

And then he would be able to go home to be with his children and his dogs. And Emma... His home. His family.

It felt like the first time in his adult life that Adam wanted to be at home as much as he wanted to be at work.

Or was that unfair?

The twins had only been babies and then toddlers while Tania had been alive. Even with the help of a nanny it had been exhausting. It was no wonder that she'd demanded to be spoilt in the times he wasn't at work. To be taken out for a candlelit dinner or away to Edinburgh or London for a shopping spree. Away from home. Away from Braeburn. Away from their children…

But he couldn't deny that it had felt so much more *like* a family since Emma had come into their lives. There was music in the house. A Christmas tree in the living room. Secrets being planned and the excitement of the upcoming Christmas production that was making life crazily busy all of a sudden.

The idea came to him from somewhere out of left field.

Did Emma really love being here as much as she seemed to?

Could she be persuaded to stay *longer*?

It wasn't fear that made his heart rate pick up this time. It was something far more positive but still enough to make him feel oddly nervous. Hope, perhaps?

Amazingly, the snow hadn't been enough to stop the playing of the pipes that Emma was coming to rely on as being a highlight of her new daily routine. It had stopped falling for the moment and the roads were still clear but it was breathtakingly cold and she couldn't sit on the bench because it would be damp even if she swept off the thin white covering.

The village centre was busy. There was a delicious smell coming from the bakery and a cluster of people outside the general store. The women saw her walk past and, instead of pretending not to, one of them nodded in her direction. The acknowledgement came without a smile but it was enough to make Emma grin and wave back. Maybe if she stopped wearing her silly Tibetan hat, she would get a smile next time.

The pipes sounded a little strange today. Had it been

harder to warm them up because it was so cold? Sharon would say that some of those notes sounded like a cat being skinned alive and she wouldn't be far wrong.

No wonder the man in the kilt stopped and lowered his instrument to stare at it in dismay.

But…to drop it?

Emma was just registering how wrong the scene in front of her was when she saw the man crumple and fall. Dropping her guitar case, she ran towards him. She'd done a first-aid course before she'd got sick herself. She knew to turn him over and check to see if he was breathing and try to see if he had a pulse.

To start CPR and shout for help.

'Get Dr McAllister,' she heard someone shout. 'Tell him it's Old Jock who needs him.'

'Call an ambulance,' someone else said. 'He looks right poorly…'

It didn't seem like any time at all until the gathering crowd of onlookers parted for Adam's arrival. He was out of breath and carrying his bag in one hand and a large piece of equipment in the other. His ferocious-looking receptionist wasn't far behind either, cradling an oxygen cylinder in her arms.

'You're doing a good job, Emma. Can you keep it up while I get organised?'

'Sure.' Emma ignored the pain from the icy cobbles beneath her knees. She bit her lip and concentrated on where she had her hands—in the middle of the chest—and how hard and fast to push.

Had it been only a matter of weeks ago that expending this much energy would have been impossible? She just had to keep it up. The last thing Adam needed right now was to have someone else collapsing.

'Okay—stop for a moment.' The buttons on the man's

waistcoat popped as Adam ripped it open. The buttons on a shirt went the same way but the singlet beneath needed a cut with shears before it would tear. And then Adam attached sticky pads to the bony chest and turned to look at the screen on the equipment he'd brought.

'Move right back, Emma. Make sure you're not touching him. I'm going to give him a shock.'

Emma—and all those watching—got a shock as well, seeing the body jerk in front of them, but she didn't have time to wallow in feeling horrified.

'Start compressions again,' Adam ordered.

'I can help the lassie.' A big man was kneeling beside her. 'I've learned how to do this.'

'Good man, Bryan. Emma—can you hold this, please? And come up by his head. I need a hand to get a tube in so we can breathe for him.'

The next few minutes were a blur. How could Adam stay so calm? He slipped a tube down the man's throat and attached it to a bag that he showed Emma how to squeeze. He put an IV line into an arm and drew up and administered drugs without any discernible shake to his hands.

Emma was shaking like a leaf now from a combination of the horror and the cold.

'Can someone ring and find out how far away the ambulance is?'

'They're sending a helicopter,' someone said moments later. 'It's going to land on the school field. They need people to check that there are no loose objects the snow might be hiding.'

Several people peeled away from the anxious group. 'We'll do that,' a man called. 'And warn the bairns what's going to happen.'

Emma fought off a wave of dizziness. She focused on

holding the bag and squeezing it. Counting to ten slowly and then squeezing it again.

'You're doing really well.'

The words were quiet. Only Emma and the big man doing the compressions would have heard it. Bryan didn't look up from his task but Emma did. She met Adam's dark gaze and found encouragement there. Pride even?

She had to swallow an unexpected lump in her throat.

'Do…do we need to send someone to find blankets? It's s-so cold…'

'It's a good thing for Old Jock,' Adam said. 'Sometimes we make patients cold deliberately to protect them from the effects of a cardiac arrest.' He looked away. 'I'll take over in a sec, Bryan. Stand clear, both of you, now. I'm going to try another shock.'

Everyone had to be holding their breath to account for the silence that followed after the warning alarm and then the clunk of the machine delivering its charge. They could hear the beat of the approaching helicopter. And then another sound, much closer. A steady blip, blip, blip that was coming from the machine.

'Is that…?'

'Aye.' Adam caught her gaze again. 'We still need to help him with his breathing but we've got a heartbeat.'

There was triumph in those eyes now. Joy even. A ripple ran through the onlookers that suggested pride in their local doctor. Confirmation that their trust in him was not misplaced.

And then the helicopter crew was there, in their bright overalls and with even more equipment. Old Jock was put onto a stretcher.

'Can you come with us, Doc?'

'Of course.' But Adam turned back to Emma. 'I have

no idea when I'll get home. It could be tricky finding transport back from Edinburgh.'

'I could come and get you.'

'What about the children? It'll be too late to be dragging them out.'

'I can take the bairns,' a woman said. 'It's no problem.' She smiled at Emma. 'I'm Jeannie's mother. Jeannie's Poppy's friend. She'd love to have a sleepover.'

Emma saw the look on Adam's face. He never asked these people for help, did he? She could understand that he might want to protect his fierce independence but these were *his* people. They cared about him just as much as he obviously cared about them.

'Leave it with me,' she told him. 'I'll call you.'

How ironic was it that she was practising the run to the big hospital in Edinburgh, having only made her arrangements with Jack hours before?

Fate seemed to be stepping in again. It had been so easy to arrange care for the children. A very excited Poppy had gone home with Jeannie for the night and Oliver was having his first-ever sleepover at his friend Ben's house.

It made it easy to ask Adam what she needed to ask, after the initial conversation and reassurance that Jock was getting the best treatment possible had faded into silence.

Thank goodness Adam was driving. Emma had used up every ounce of energy she had and she knew she would fall asleep very soon. Maybe it was sheer exhaustion that stopped her feeling hesitant in making her request.

'Would it be all right if I had a day off next week?

I've…got a kind of appointment in Edinburgh that I need to go to.'

'Of course you can have a day off. You haven't had one since you came. I keep telling you I can cope at the weekends.'

'The thing is…it's a weekday, not the weekend, and I'd need to stay the night. The…ah…appointment's late so I'd need to wait until the next day to get the train back. It would be fine for the children to stay with their friends again. I…um…checked.'

The sideways look she received was disconcerting. It reminded her of that first time she'd met Adam, when he'd looked at her as if she was the last person he'd want to be looking after his children. The atmosphere in the car suddenly felt like it had on that first day, too, when he'd driven her home and she'd been imagining his wife buried somewhere under the driveway.

It did sound dodgy, didn't it? A late-night appointment? And it was on a day that would make child care a challenge for him and she'd taken a huge liberty in tentatively making arrangements herself. But she couldn't tell him the truth or he might realise he *had* made a mistake in trusting her with his children. That she was sick and…and unreliable.

'It's a…job interview…' she heard herself saying. Unconvincingly? She tried again. 'Music's my first love. That's why I don't take on full-time or permanent jobs. I'm seeing someone about the possibility of a future gig.'

That wasn't so far from the truth, was it? It was just about her whole future and not just a gig.

The silence kept growing. Becoming more and more loaded with every passing second, but Adam was being assaulted by unpleasant emotions.

Had he really thought Emma was incapable of lying? It was *obvious* she was not telling the truth right now. He could hear echoes of Tania.

There's a sale on... It's my favourite designer, darling... It's only for a day...maybe two...

But it wasn't fair not to trust Emma because of the skill with which Tania had manipulated him.

He wanted to trust her. So much.

And it wasn't her fault that it was so hard.

Finally—too late—he managed a grunt in response. But he couldn't meet her eyes. He had to keep staring at the road ahead of them.

'Do what you need to,' he growled. 'I'll cope.'

Emma woke up as the car jolted over the tree roots on the driveway and, almost instantly, found herself shivering.

It wasn't just the physical cold, although there was enough snow now for her feet to crunch through it as she followed Adam up the steps to the front door.

This was an emotional chill, too.

Adam McAllister had gone back into his shell, hadn't he? Back to being the man who never really smiled and who couldn't bear the celebration of something as joyous as Christmas.

And all because she'd asked for a day off?

No. Emma knew there was more to it than that. Maybe it was the way Adam was avoiding both eye contact and any conversation as they went into the house. Or it could have been the way Bob shot her an almost accusing look before going quietly to his master's side. Most likely, it was catching sight of the mistletoe wreath that Emma had hung in the corner near the coat stand that made it crystal clear.

This was about the kiss.

About *her*.

The desire wasn't one-sided, was it? But Adam didn't know what to do about it because he was still caught in his grief and she'd just made it clear that she couldn't wait to move on—to another *gig*.

For once Adam wasn't rushing into the kitchen where he'd drop his coat over the back of the nearest chair or on the arm of the sofa. He was taking it off slowly and deliberately and clearly intended hanging it on the rack.

Slowly enough for Emma to have another blinding moment of clarity.

She'd thought she had nothing to offer Adam but she had been wrong.

Catherine would applaud the fact that she'd pushed him into allowing Christmas into his house for the sake of the children but...what if she could give him—give *all* of them—more than that?

This man deserved to be loved again.

The children desperately needed a mother, not just a series of nannies.

How perfect would it be if it could be her?

But, if it couldn't, she could still help. She could help him take that first step. They had the house to themselves. Nobody but she and Adam need know.

Maybe the real gift she could give Adam was the permission to be really happy again? To show him what it *could* be like.

She could offer Adam hope. A belief that it was possible. He was an outstanding doctor and father but she could help him get over that huge barrier he'd put around himself as a man.

'Adam?' Slipping out of her own coat, Emma stood beside him at the coat rack. 'I'm sorry... I don't have to go to that appointment in Edinburgh. It's not that I don't want to be here with you and children. It's just that—'

'It doesn't matter. I told you that.'

'But it does,' Emma said softly. 'I don't want to make things difficult. I know I'm not here for very long but I want this to be a special time—one that will make special memories—for all of us...'

Herself included. The whisper in the back of her mind reminded her that this could turn out to be her last Christmas. She had nothing to lose. Adam had everything to gain.

Oh, help...he was standing so very still. His eyes were closed.

When his eyes slowly opened, he wasn't looking down at Emma. He was looking up—at the mistletoe wreath. And then he reached up and picked a whole bunch of those little, waxy white berries.

Finally, he made eye contact and the smouldering depths in those dark eyes stole Emma's breath.

And her heart.

He might be fighting it but he *wanted* her.

Needed her.

Emma had to close her eyes because her own wanting and needing was overwhelming and this had to be Adam's decision. His choice.

She heard his deep groan. And then she felt him move. One arm went around her waist and the other caught the back of her legs. She was scooped up as if she weighed almost nothing and she held on tightly and buried her face against his neck, allowing herself to sink into total trust as Adam carried her upstairs.

To his bed.

* * *

She felt so light in his arms. Thin enough to seem fragile as he set her down gently onto her feet when he'd reached his room and pushed the door shut with his foot to keep the dogs out.

To keep the whole world out.

Emma's arms were still around his neck as her feet touched the floor and she must have stayed on tiptoe to reach his lips with her own so easily.

There was nothing fragile about that kiss. He could feel only the strength of her desire and a need that was as great as his own for the comfort of intimate, human touch.

It had been *so* long. Adam's hands slipped beneath the woollen jumper to feel skin that was like silk. Small, firm breasts that seemed to push themselves into his hands and nipples that were as hard as tiny pebbles.

Touching them with his hands wasn't enough. Not nearly enough. As blissful as it was, kissing Emma, he needed his mouth and his lips to savour other parts of her perfect body.

A tug on her clothing seemed to be enough. Emma dropped her arms and stepped back. Just far enough to grasp her jumper herself and peel it off over her head. And then she began to unbutton her shirt but Adam stilled her hands.

'Let me.'

His fingers fumbled with the tiny buttons and Adam realised, to his horror, that they were shaking. She wasn't watching his hands, though. As he looked up he found she was watching his face. Waiting for a contact that went so much deeper than physical touch. And when he gave it to her, he couldn't look away.

Could he do this? Could he love Emma in the way she deserved to be loved? Without disappointing her?

Emma could feel the tears in her eyes as she felt the way Adam's hands were trembling.

This big, strong man who could save a life and do such intricate manoeuvres with those hands without the slightest tremor couldn't hide his emotions in this moment.

This was huge. So huge that Adam was nervous. It wouldn't last. She knew that as soon as they got over this awkward moment of shedding their clothing and they could touch each other properly, any doubts or nerves on either side would cease to exist.

But in this brief moment of such vulnerability she realised just how much she loved Adam. She wouldn't only be giving him her body tonight. She would be giving him her heart—for as long as he wanted it.

Or as long as fate would allow.

And maybe something of what she was feeling was communicated as they held each other's gaze for such a long, long moment, because she felt that trembling stop. She saw the doubt vanish from Adam's eyes and could see something that seemed to mirror what she was feeling herself. A reflection—or was Adam gifting her *his* heart?

And then she could see—or maybe sense—the moment that desire ignited and there was nothing but the need to be as close as physically possible. There was no further awkwardness. Anything that was going to stop them being skin to skin seemed to be discarded as easily as ice melting in hot sunshine.

Adam flicked back the bed covers and then drew Emma against his body. In a heartbeat they would be lying on that bed together but she loved it that he stopped to gaze at her for a moment longer. To bend his head and give her such a tender kiss that promised he would look after her.

That he intended to make this night unforgettable.

Not that Emma had the slightest doubt that this would be the case but she loved being given the promise. Along with her body and her heart, Adam McAllister had just won her lifelong trust.

CHAPTER EIGHT

THE MAGIC WAS getting stronger.

Emma's gift to Adam had been received so well it seemed that he wanted to unwrap it all over again the following night, and Emma was only too happy to participate, tiptoeing into Adam's room when the children were fast asleep.

How amazing that the same gift could be given in both directions.

And that parts of it could be given to others without them knowing how or why it was happening?

They were being very careful to make sure the children didn't realise what had changed between them but the magic was still happening.

The new connection between Adam and Emma was sending out tendrils that were touching the children. Making them all feel like a family.

Like when naughty Benji had mistaken the old teddy Poppy carried everywhere now, for a dog toy and had grabbed its leg. Poppy had tried to keep hold of it but ended up pulling off the damaged arm and she had been distraught.

'Emma can fix it,' Adam consoled her.

'Daddy can fix it,' Emma said at the same time.

They looked at each other and smiled.

'You're good at sewing,' Adam said. 'I've seen that pretty dress you made Poppy for the play.'

'You're the doctor,' she said solemnly. 'An amputated arm is much more in your line of work.'

'Aye...' Adam nodded thoughtfully but his eyes held a mischievous glint. 'I'll need a scrub nurse, though.'

'I love new jobs.' It was hard not to grin but Poppy was still sobbing.

'We need a clean sheet,' Adam told her, 'so we've got an operating table. Ollie? Can you go and bring my doctor bag, please?'

It was a treat, turning the small disaster into a game that the children were fascinated by. With a clean sheet on the table, Adam pretended to give teddy an anaesthetic with a nebuliser. He'd found masks and gloves for both he and Emma to wear and he seemed more than happy to use up other medical supplies, like the suture kit.

It might have been a game but watching Adam draw the teddy's furry fabric together and make the complicated-looking knots of real sutures impressed Emma as much as it did the children. Their father was doing his important, *real* work at home. For teddy.

'Pay attention, scrub nurse,' Adam growled at one point. 'You have to cut the thread now.'

Emma giggled and, after a startled moment, so did both the children.

Teddy's arm got bandaged when the operation was finished and then he got sent off to Intensive Care in Poppy's bedroom because it was bedtime. Ollie got to carry him because he'd been promoted to orderly.

'I'll bet they'll remember that for the rest of their lives,' Emma told Adam later that night as she lay in his arms yet again. 'The night Daddy operated on teddy.'

'I think I'll remember it,' Adam replied quietly. 'It was special.'

'Magic,' Emma agreed happily.

'Aye…' Adam bent his head to kiss her again. 'Like you…'

The newest member of the Braeburn McAllister clan was born in the new light of the day after teddy's surgery.

Everyone in the village assumed that was why Dr McAllister was looking so happy. He had a bonny new niece and everybody was fine and his mother would head home in a couple of weeks and life would carry on just the same but better.

'They've called the wee lassie Holly—did you hear? Because she's been born sae close to Christmas.'

If anyone wondered why that Miss Sinclair seemed to be just as happy as the rest of the family, even though she was no relation to the new bairn, they just gave each other knowing looks. She was always a happy wee thing, wasn't she? A bit different, mind, with strange clothes and carrying her guitar with her everywhere, but you couldn't say a word against how she looked after those twins and the way she was getting involved with the school's Christmas production and even with the fund-raising for the hall committee.

And, oh, my…she *could* sing like a wee angel, couldn't she?

Phone calls and texts and photographs pinged between Scotland and Canada but it was a couple of days before everything came together well enough for a family gathering, courtesy of an online video chat.

Marion and Holly were back home already with Ian—the proud husband and new father—and Catherine was using her tablet. Adam had set up his desktop computer in the living room. With a fire burning merrily in the grate and the lights on the Christmas tree twinkling, it seemed the perfect background for a digital reunion, but Catherine McAllister seemed overwhelmed by the initial visual contact.

'Oh…is that a…a…*Christmas* tree?'

'It's *our* Christmas tree, Gran…' Poppy leaned in close to the computer screen to make sure her grandmother could see her properly. 'Emma helped us paint the balls and we sticked the sweets on the stars and we made paper chains and…and *everything*.'

Catherine probably couldn't see anything except Poppy's nose, Emma thought, but there was no mistaking the pride and joy the small girl was radiating. She could see the screen but she was staying out of range of the camera, sitting on the floor near the fire, flanked by Bob and Benji.

There was no mistaking the voice thickened by tears from the other end of the connection either.

'That's wonderful, darling. It's the most beautiful Christmas tree I've ever seen. Emma's clever, isn't she?'

'Aye.' Adam gently pulled Poppy's head back to allow a wider camera view. 'She's made a dress for Poppy, too. For the school play. I told you that Jemima's going to be in the production, didn't I?'

Laughter came from behind Catherine and the picture on the screen changed angles sharply. They got a view of polished wooden floorboards and then feet and then the picture settled on a young woman sitting in an armchair with a small bundle in her arms. She could be Adam's twin, not just his sister, Emma thought. With that same dark hair and eyes and a smile that was so like Adam's when he was really happy.

She'd seen that smile so often in the last few days. Everyone had and it was contagious. There was so much laughter in this house now and even people in the village seemed to be smiling more.

'Are you trying to upstage me, Adam? Creating havoc in the village so nobody's got time to talk about my wee Holly? Whose crazy idea was it to take our donkey into the hall?'

'*Emma's*,' the twins chorused.

Oliver pushed past Poppy to take centre stage. 'Aunty Marion—can you come and see our play? I'm going to be Joseph and I get to lead Jemima until we get to the stage and I've got a…a rib that Emma made out of a sheet—'

'Robe,' Adam supplied.

'And I wear a stripy tea towel on my head and Emma's made a special rope thing to hold it on and…'

And Marion was laughing again. 'I can't come this time, pet. I have to be here to look after wee Holly. But *next* year we'll all be back in Braeburn and we'll all come and see the play.'

'But Jemima won't be in it next year.'

And I won't be here, Emma thought. She had to dip her head and swallow hard.

'I think I need to meet this Emma,' Marion declared. 'Where is she?'

'She's here.' Adam turned away from the computer and held out his hand. 'Come over, Emma. Come and meet my sister and our new niece.'

She couldn't not respond to that outstretched hand. To the invitation in those eyes and the smile she was coming to love more and more. With the children standing in front of them, nobody would notice that Adam caught her hand when she got close enough, would they? Or that he laced his fingers through hers and kept holding it as Emma smiled at the screen.

'Hi, Marion. Congratulations. I've seen the pictures of Holly and she's just gorgeous.'

Adam squeezed her hand and it was automatic to look up and return his smile. Hard to look away quickly enough to avoid making it obvious that her relationship with her employer had undergone a radical change recently.

Marion looked away from the screen for a moment, her face a question mark. Was she exchanging a significant look with her mother? But then she was smiling again, possibly even more widely than before.

'I hear you can sing,' she said. 'That you—and the children of Braeburn school—are about to become rich and famous.'

Emma laughed. 'I don't think so. But a local radio station got hold of the story about us making a CD of Christmas carols as a fundraiser. They've organised a bus to take us all into a recording studio and they're going to make it available as a download so lots of people can buy it. With a bit of luck, we'll be able to fix up the hall *and* get a new piano for the school.'

The twins were feeling left out.

'I've got a train, Aunty Marion. It's on the floor by the tree, see?'

'No, I can't see it, pet.'

'I'll get the engine and *show* you.' Oliver wriggled between Adam and Emma and they had to break their handhold.

'And I've got a bear.' Poppy held it up and pressed it against the computer screen. 'Benji pulled him and the arm felled off but Daddy and Emma poperated it and it's all better now.'

'Good heavens…that's *my* old bear,' came Catherine's voice.

'We found it in the attic when we went up to hunt out the Christmas decorations,' Adam explained. 'You don't mind, do you? Ollie's train was the one I had when I was his age. I'd forgotten it was even there.'

'Of course I don't mind.' Catherine's eyes were suspiciously bright. 'It's wonderful that you found things to use again. Oh…I wish I was there with you. You all look *so* happy.'

If they hadn't noticed anything significant in the glance Adam and Emma had exchanged before, they would surely pick up on something this time as Adam turned to Emma and smiled.

'We are,' he said.

'But what on earth did you do to the bear to fix it?'

'A poperation,' Poppy shouted. 'I *told* you.'

'An *operation*.' Emma was laughing. 'Daddy got a special needle and thread from his doctor's bag and sewed teddy's arm back on.'

'I growled at Benji,' Poppy added. 'And he looked sad.'

'Is Benji going to be in the play, too?' Marion asked.

''Course not.' Oliver was back with the train engine. 'He's a *dog*.'

'Maybe he could pretend to be a sheep?'

'No.' Adam shook his head. 'Don't go putting ideas in their heads, Miri. You're as bad as Emma. We've got more than enough going on right now. I'm helping to shift hay bales into the hall tomorrow. Bryan from the pub is making a manger.'

The connection crackled and the picture pixelated for a moment. By the time it cleared, baby Holly was crying and it was hard to hear conversation.

'We'd better go,' Adam said. 'It's very late for you.

We'll try again on Christmas Day, aye? Children—come and blow a kiss to your wee cousin.'

With a chorus of 'Miss you' and 'Love you lots' the call ended. For a moment the blankness of the screen seemed to dampen the atmosphere in the room.

Emma groaned. 'Oh, no…we forgot to sing the carol for the baby.'

The twins were good at speaking in unison. 'Deck the halls with boughs of *holly*…'

They were also good at looking equally disappointed.

'Never mind. We needed to practise a bit more anyway. We'll be extra-good at it for Christmas Day.'

But Poppy's lip wobbled and Oliver hugged the train engine more tightly.

'It's almost bedtime but why don't we have a quick practice now? Maybe Daddy could record it on his phone and we could *send* it to Gran and Aunty Marion.'

'I'll get your kit-ar,' Poppy offered.

'No.' Oliver glared at her. 'That's *my* job.'

Happiness had been restored yet again, thanks to Emma's way of dealing with problems.

No. Maybe it was being created rather than restored.

That was certainly the case for Adam, he realised much later that night as he held Emma in his arms yet again.

She was asleep but he pressed a gentle kiss to the top of her head and the pressure seemed to bounce back in a shaft that went straight to his chest, where it encased his heart and squeezed it tightly.

Was this what happiness felt like?

But this was something he'd never felt before and he knew there had been times he'd been happy. His childhood had been a happy one. He'd been secure and loved and he'd had friends and he'd loved school and his music lessons. It had been Old Jock who'd taught him to play the bagpipes and he'd been so proud that Christmastime when his pupil had been chosen to be the lone piper for the school production. He'd never said anything to Adam in the years since he'd stopped playing but he knew how happy the old man would be if he confessed that he was ready to pick up his pipes again.

Thank goodness Emma had been there and had known what to do the other day. Jock had been very lucky. He might have still survived his cardiac arrest but it had to be thanks to good-quality CPR that he'd come through without any neurological damage.

Gratitude added another layer to Adam's sense of well-being and his breath came out in a soft sigh.

It wasn't just Jock who was lucky that Emma had come to Braeburn.

His children were as happy as he'd ever seen them. Maybe it was partly due to the festive decorations that seemed to be creeping into every corner of the house. Today's addition had been big tartan bows at intervals all the way up the bannisters on the stairs. Or maybe it wasn't the decorations so much as his giving permission to *have* them?

Had he shut happiness out of the house without intending to? Had it just become a habit because he'd lived with his grief and his guilt for so long?

That he was letting go was thanks to Emma, too. She'd come here with her music and songs and…and her sheer *joie de vivre* and she'd given them all something that could never have been wrapped and put under a Christmas tree.

What was it that was creating this feeling that was almost euphoria?

Part of it was the kind of excitement he remembered from when he'd been a child. On Christmas morning when he would tiptoe downstairs before anyone else was awake to see if the magic had happened and there were mysterious, brightly wrapped parcels under the tree.

Part of it was hope. The kind of hope he'd felt when he'd persuaded Tania to marry him and come to live in his own little patch of the world? He'd thought that he'd never feel that kind of hope again. The one that suggested that he'd found all that he needed to keep him happy for the rest of his life. He'd been wrong that time but the hope had never been this strong, had it? It was time to put it all behind him. Time to take off the wedding ring that symbolised his entrapment in the past?

And Adam knew that part of it was also love. Maybe the biggest part. The kind of love he'd felt when he'd held his newborn babies for the first time. That almost desperate urge to protect them. To hold them and cherish them. For ever. He felt that urge about Emma now and it made him stroke her skin very lightly. Over her shoulder and along her collar bone. She had a tiny scar that interrupted the perfection of her smooth skin. Funny place for a scar—almost exactly where someone would have a central line inserted for a major medical procedure. He'd have to ask her some time how it came to be.

Emma shifted in his arms and made a tiny sound. She would wake soon. Maybe they would make love again. Even the thought of it stirred desire but Adam didn't want her to wake just yet because he knew she wouldn't sleep in his arms again tonight. She would creep back to her own room so that the children wouldn't know she hadn't been there all night.

To protect him—in case they said something at school

and then the whole village would know what was going on in the McAllister house?

Maybe it was to protect them—so that they wouldn't get ideas that Emma might be in their lives for ever?

If they asked, he might tell them that he hoped she might be but hope wasn't something to give lightly. He'd seen it in his mother's face tonight. And his sister's.

In the way they'd looked at each other as if they knew what was going on between him and Emma.

He would have seen it in his own face in the mirror all those years ago, when he'd been getting dressed for his wedding.

Hope was fragile. Like a glass bubble that could shatter all too easily. He hadn't intended ever trying to hold one himself again but it had formed without him really noticing.

And now it was here.

And it was huge.

The days were passing in a blur.

There was so much to do. Emma had never been so busy in her life but she was loving every minute of it. Final rehearsals for the school's Christmas production that would happen on Christmas Eve were in full swing. The junior-school trip to the recording studio had happened yesterday on the last day of school and the CDs were due to arrive today. There had been a picture of them all in the newspaper and already there were apparently orders coming in and people waiting to download the amateur production. Women in the village were not only smiling at Emma, they were *talking* to her. This was the most exciting thing that had happened in Braeburn since...

They never said what else had happened that was so

exciting but Emma had to wonder if it had been when their beloved doctor had brought his beautiful young wife home to his village.

Funny how a ghost could cast such a shadow but it wasn't the only shadow Emma was aware of today.

The arrangements were all in place. Poppy was spending the day with Jeannie and Oliver was with Ben. Their mothers would take them to the play practice later and Caitlin had offered to take Poppy to her dance class, where they were also doing a final rehearsal for their upcoming appearance, and Adam would collect her. He would also take Oliver to his music lesson tomorrow morning to prepare for the junior pipers' display. The Christmas Eve school production wasn't just a nativity play from the youngest pupils. It was more like a talent show. A celebration of everything the village children had accomplished for their year.

Nobody seemed to mind that Emma was skipping town for a day and a night. She would be back in time. The knowing looks and veiled comments she'd received had let her know that they thought she was really going to Edinburgh to do some Christmas shopping. The way Mrs McAllister used to. And didn't the bairns deserve something special? Their poor father never had the time to go far afield to create Christmas surprises but Emma was good at surprises, wasn't she?

Oh, yes…the shadows were gathering and, as she sat alone in the train on the way to Edinburgh, they formed a black cloud that threatened a storm.

Had she made a terrible mistake in trying to create a perfect Christmas for the McAllister family? For herself?

She hadn't intended falling in love with Adam but it had happened. And, if this was going to be her last Christmas, how magical was it to feel this happy?

This *loved*.

She hadn't intended to give Adam any more than the reminder of what it was like to let a woman close. To help him step forward from his grief. She hadn't expected him to fall in love with *her*. Not that he'd said anything but she could feel it in every touch. Every kiss. She could see it in his eyes when she turned unexpectedly and found him looking at her.

What if she'd set him up to suffer loss all over again?

And at *Christmas*time?

No. She couldn't afford to let a single bolt of lightning detach itself from that storm cloud. Jack was waiting for her to arrive at the infirmary. She would have the horrible test this afternoon, sleep off the effects of the drugs and then go back to Braeburn and enjoy every moment of this Christmas.

She had to remember to post the CD she had burned last night, too. Not that it would reach Sharon by Christmas Day, of course, but that was okay. The collection of photographs and the song she had written for her best friend would arrive electronically on the right day. The CD was just a back-up. She'd made one for herself as well.

It was snowing again by the time Emma carried her small bag into the brightly lit entrance to the huge hospital. There was a massive Christmas tree in the foyer, covered in silver decorations—like theirs would have been if she and the children hadn't painted all those balls. The girl at the reception desk was wearing a bright badge that had Rudolf the reindeer with a flashing red nose. Even the telephone she picked up to page Jack with was wrapped in tinsel.

And Jack's smile when he saw her looked like Christmas. So warm. Full of hope? His hug was comforting.

'Let's get this over with, Emma. Are you ready?'

Emma could only nod. Her throat felt tight and tears stung the back of her eyes. Hope was like a bubble, wasn't it?

A freshly blown one that caught all the colours of the rainbow and was so pretty that you wanted to catch it and keep it.

But it would only break if you tried.

CHAPTER NINE

THE HUM OF conversation stopped. Even the small girls stopped skipping about and giggling.

'Dr McAllister... What's happened?'

'Nothing's happened. I'm just here to collect Poppy.'

'Where's Emma?'

'She had to go to Edinburgh. She'll be back tomorrow afternoon.'

'Oh...thank goodness for that.' The young mothers shared relieved glances. 'She's not going to miss the performance, then. It wouldn't be the same, would it, without her singing with the children?'

'No.'

The mothers turned their attention to getting their daughters to change their shoes and put coats and hats on before going out into the snow. Having got over the surprise of seeing him at the dance class, nobody seemed to expect Adam to say anything else. People drifted away, leaving him alone with Poppy as he helped her with the laces on her dancing shoes. Because they were so used to giving him the space he'd always demanded by keeping people at a distance? Odd that it felt a little...disappointing?

At least the teacher came to talk to him.

'Did ye get the note, Dr McAllister? About the kilt?'

'Aye…' There had been a note, hadn't there? Weeks ago. Kylie had said something about needing to order a kilt for Poppy for her first dance performance but that had been about the time that his previous nanny had announced her pregnancy and intention of emigrating to Australia and life had suddenly become chaotic. He'd totally forgotten about it.

The teacher gave him a sympathetic smile. 'It's no' essential,' she said. 'I'm sure Poppy's got a skirt she could wear. We can give her a tartan sash.'

'But I want a kilt,' Poppy said. She tugged on her father's sleeve. 'I *love* kilts, Daddy.'

'We'll find you a kilt, pet, I promise.'

How he was going to manage to keep that promise within the next forty-eight hours was beyond Adam at the moment but there were other things to deal with first. Like getting the children home and fed. Looking after the dogs and collecting the eggs from the hens and making sure Jemima had plenty of fresh hay. Poppy took the little donkey a carrot.

'You're going to be in our play,' she said happily. 'You have to be very good and then you'll get more carrots.'

'She *will* have to be very good,' Adam agreed. He couldn't help shaking his head as a wave of bemusement caught him off guard. Were they really going to transport Jemima into the village hall to star in the nativity play?

Extraordinary.

As astonishing as the person who'd made it happen, in fact.

Emma's absence in the house that evening was far more noticeable than Adam had expected. It wasn't just that he had so much more that he needed to do. Everywhere he turned, he could see things that made him think of Emma. The paper chains hanging from the beams in the kitchen. The Christmas tree in the living room. The children asking for songs instead of a bedtime story.

He did his best but it wasn't the same.

'It's okay,' Oliver said kindly. 'Emma will be back tomorrow.'

It wasn't just the lack of music in the house that made it feel oddly quiet. The atmosphere was different. Emma didn't have to be singing, did she? She only had to be present for there to be a unique energy in the house.

A promise of something good.

Joy, perhaps.

Or love…

To distract himself from what was missing, Adam went online to check out the availability of kilts for small girls. But even that reminded him of Emma. Of the conversation in the kitchen that first weekend she'd been here. When she'd asked him if there was a McAllister tartan and whether he ever wore a kilt.

He'd been terse, hadn't he? Pushed her away, the way he always did when people got too close. It worked so well because they understood why he needed his space. Or they thought they did.

Emma hadn't respected those boundaries, though. She'd pushed until he could see them for what they were. Prison bars keeping him in the past. Hurting his children.

He found a specialist shop and clicked on the Clan Donald tartan. There was a children's section and he found a clan kilt in a new tartan that had been designed in recent years. With a purple background and small gold, red and green stripes, it was far more feminine than the dark colours of the kilt he had hanging in his own wardrobe. It would be perfect for Poppy. It seemed to be in stock in the right size but could they deliver it in time? Adam took note of the phone number. He'd give them a call tomorrow morning after he'd dropped Ollie at his music lesson.

With his hands still hovering over the keyboard, Adam caught the glint that the screen light coaxed from the dull gold band on his finger. It wasn't just the personal barriers he'd erected that were prison bars keeping him in the past, was it?

With a movement familiar enough to be automatic he used his thumb to touch the metal. Did he rub it as a reassuring link to a past he wasn't permitted to forget or was he actually trying to hide it?

On impulse, he closed the fingers of his right hand over the ring and gave it a tug. It didn't budge. He tried twisting it and it moved a little. Enough to make him get up abruptly and startle the dogs, who followed him curiously into the bathroom where he lathered his hands with soap until he could move the ring more freely. It took some effort to get it over his knuckle but—suddenly—it was off.

He was holding the symbol of his past and his failed marriage and the tragedy of losing his wife and... And he had no idea what to do with it now. The thought of taking it up the back of Old Jock's farm and hurling it into the pond was appealing. Just as well it was so late and the pond was frozen over anyway. Back in the library to shut down the computer, Adam dropped the ring into a drawer of his desk.

Walking up the stairs to bed, he was again aware of Emma's absence and this time it came with a yearning ache because he was going to his bed alone. He paused for a moment, in the spot where he'd first heard the haunting notes of that song coming from her room late at night, catching his breath as he realised how much he was missing her.

His left hand was curled, his thumb rubbing the empty place where the ring had been. There was nothing there to touch. Nothing to hide.

Or should that be no*where* to hide?

It wouldn't be long before someone noticed that he'd taken his ring off. Eileen's sharp eyes didn't miss a thing. There would be talk, of course, but he suspected that the consensus of the village women would be that three years' mourning was more than enough. He had done his duty and upheld the myth that the marriage had been too perfect to move on from and he'd done it for long enough to ensure that the children were protected. They would always have their 'angel' mother but they deserved more than that in their lives. Someone real, who made their lives more joyful.

Would the villagers go further and speculate how much influence Emma's presence had had on his decision?

Probably.

Did he mind?

If he did, he'd get used to it—the way he had got used to carrying the burden of the truth alone. Maybe—hopefully—he'd have to, because he had made more than one decision tonight. He was going to ask Emma to stay in Braeburn longer and he was pretty confident that she would agree. He'd had the strong impression today that she didn't really want to go. She'd seemed reluctant to even go to that job interview in the end. And it was good that she had gone because it gave her options. And if she chose to stay, it would be because she really wanted to.

If she did want to stay, he could start hoping for something more permanent. Not just for the children—he wanted that for himself as well.

* * *

The hotel in Edinburgh was a lovely old sandstone building that had been close enough to the hospital to make it the ideal place for Emma to spend the night and sleep off the effects of the drugs she'd been given for her procedure.

Not that she'd slept particularly well. Despite being only two days before Christmas, the hotel was very quiet, which should have been a bonus but it made Emma feel lonely. She missed the sound of children nearby. Even more, she missed being near Adam. So much that it was a physical ache that had nothing to do with the holes that had been bored into her hip bone. She longed for the sound of his voice. The way his presence filled a room. Just a shared look would have been enough—to see the warmth in those gorgeous, dark eyes and the promise that always seemed to be there now.

Oh…help. It was going to be very hard to leave, wasn't it?

At least she could distract herself with some Christmas shopping this morning. She wanted to find something special for Poppy and Oliver. And for Adam. Something that they'd keep for ever and it would remind them of her?

She needed something for Jack as well. He'd gone to a lot of effort to ensure she didn't have the results of this test as a dark cloud hanging over her future for any longer than was absolutely necessary and, as usual, he'd done his best to make the procedure as painless as possible. A bottle of really nice Scotch, perhaps? She could give it to him later because they'd arranged to meet in the hospital café for a coffee before she drove back to Braeburn. Just a quick check, Jack had said—to see that there were no complications from the test. And the results of the blood tests would be back by then, although the examination of her bone marrow would take up to seven days. From past experience, however, Emma knew that the preliminary results could arrive within forty eight hours and, so far, they'd always been an accurate prediction of what lay ahead.

It was a bit painful to walk this morning but a couple of painkillers along with her breakfast and she'd be fine to wander through the lovely boutique shops on the Royal Mile and Grassmarket. A quick coffee with Jack and then she could be on her way, heading back to Braeburn. She wished she could just get on the train and start travelling now. Not that she'd make it back in time for the big dress rehearsal of the play but at least she'd be going in the right direction.

On the way back to the people she had already come to love so deeply.

Caitlin McMurray was coping with at least fifteen over-excited children by the time Adam dropped Poppy and Oliver at the school.

'Och...here's our wee Mary and Joseph.' Caitlin looked relieved. 'Where are our shepherds? Over *here*, Jamie, thank you. No—we're not getting the paints out.' She grinned at Adam. 'Don't you love the silly season?'

Adam smiled back. 'I'm sorry I can't stay to help. I need to get to the clinic and see if anyone needs me.'

Except that he found someone who needed him even before he got as far as the clinic. Joan McClintock, almost buried in her cold-weather clothes, was standing outside the church.

'How are you, Joan?'

'Och...you know, Doctor. I've been better.'

'Still feeling peaky?'

'Aye...'

'You're sounding a bit short o' puff.' Automatically, Adam reached for Joan's hand, negotiating the heavy coat cuff and a woollen glove to find her pulse.

'Aye…I am at that. Must be the cold.'

'Come into the clinic with me. I'd like to check your blood pressure.'

'Och, I didn't want to be a bother, Dr McAllister.'

'It's no bother, Joan.' She was looking pale, Adam thought, and there was something about her that was ringing alarm bells. Made him think of Old Jock, who'd also been a bit 'short o' puff' shortly before he'd collapsed and nearly died.

There were two people in the waiting room but Eileen took one look at her friend's face and made no comment about a disruption to the morning's timetable.

'Och, Joan…you're no' looking right. It's a good thing you're here to see the doctor.'

His elderly patient's blood pressure wasn't concerning and her pulse seemed steady enough but Adam still wasn't happy.

'Is there anything else happening, Joan? You've no' got any chest pain or nausea or anything?'

'Noo… I've just… I don' *feel* right, you know?'

'Aye. I'm going to do a twelve-lead ECG.' He knew it would be a mission to get down to skin and attach all the electrodes but he wasn't going to let that deter him. It was quite possible for someone to be having a heart attack with almost no symptoms—especially a stoic, elderly woman.

Sure enough, the ECG trace showed unmistakeable evidence that Joan was, indeed, in the early stages of a heart attack. She needed to get to a hospital with catheter lab facilities as soon as possible.

'I'm going to send you into hospital,' Adam told her,

after carefully explaining what he'd found. 'The sooner you get treatment, the less damage there will be to your heart. I'll get Eileen to call an ambulance.'

'I'm no' going in any ambulance.' Joan was already pulling her clothes back on. 'I'm fine, Doctor.'

'You're not fine, Joan. Here—I want you to chew up these aspirin tablets and wash them down with some water.'

But Joan was too upset to co-operate. Her shortness of breath was increasing and Adam knew that a panic attack was not only imminent but would be the worst thing for her, given that the blood supply to her heart was already compromised.

'All right. No ambulance. I'll talk to Eileen and we'll find someone who can drive you.'

'No…' Joan's face crumpled. 'It's been snowing… it's dangerous… I don't trust *anyone*…to drive me *anywhere*…'

Her breath was coming in short gasps now and she had a hand pressed to the centre of her chest. He had to break this cycle before a catastrophe happened—but how?

Adam took hold of Joan's hand with both of his. 'Do you trust *me*, Joan?'

'Oh…aye, Doctor. Of course I do.'

'Would you let *me* drive you to the hospital?'

'But—'

'Wait here. I've going to have a wee word with Eileen and we'll get everything sorted. And then I'm going to pop a wee needle in your hand and give you something to help you relax.' He squeezed her hand. 'It's all going to be all right, Joan. You just need to let me look after you.'

Amazingly, Eileen didn't look remotely outraged at the prospect of having to reschedule the waiting patients and neither of them seemed bothered about the inconvenience. Perhaps the drama of Old Jock's narrow escape was fresh enough to have everyone watching out for each other.

'You just take care of Joan, Doctor.'

'And say hello to Jock while you're in there.'

That was a thought. He could not only check up on Jock but he could see how Aimee Jessop's baby was doing. He might even be able to pop into the specialty shop and see if he could pick up that kilt for Poppy.

'Oh…' About to head back to get Joan ready for the journey, Adam stopped in his tracks.

'Don't worry,' Eileen said. 'I'll take care of things here. If anyone's looking right poorly, I'll call an ambulance.'

'It's the children,' Adam said. 'They'll be finished their play practice by lunchtime. I'll no' be back in time to collect them.'

'I'll do that,' Eileen said. 'We'll get some lunch and they can come and play here until you get back.'

The suggestion that the children were welcome to come and play in Eileen's closely guarded domain was astonishing but Adam didn't have time to reflect on the fact that it wasn't only in his own home that things seemed to be changing. He needed to look after Joan.

Two hours later, his elderly patient was on her way to the catheter laboratory at the Royal. Adam visited Paediatrics to hear the good news that the Jessop baby was putting on weight and that her mother had been able to hold her, and then he got a surprise in the cardiology ward when he was told that Jock was well enough to go home. They were about to arrange transport.

'He can come back with me,' Adam said. 'I just need a quick coffee and a sandwich and I'll be back to collect him.'

The café at the infirmary was renowned for its good food and great coffee but Adam didn't even get as far as the queue at the counter.

At first, he simply didn't believe what he was seeing. It had to be a symptom of how much space Emma Sinclair was taking up in his head these days that made him see things in other women that reminded him of her.

The petite frame or a tumble of curly hair. Blue eyes or even a song on the radio…

But no. This time it wasn't just a glimpse of something that made him realise how special Emma was and how much he wanted to be with her.

It *was* her.

And she wasn't alone.

She was sitting at a table with a man who was roughly his own age. The way they were leaning towards each other suggested more than simply familiarity and if he'd been prepared to bestow the benefit of doubt, the inclination would have evaporated the instant he noted that they were holding hands. Staring at each other so intently there was no danger of him being noticed.

Not that the inclination to question the evidence had been there in the first place.

Emma had said she was coming to Edinburgh for a job interview and he'd believed her. Trusted her.

Had he really thought she was so completely different from his wife?

Tania had always said she came to Edinburgh to do her Christmas shopping.

He'd trusted her, too.

Were all women like this? No…he knew that wasn't true. So it had to be something to do with *him*. And whatever failing he had, it was accompanied by a blindness he'd never imagined he'd have to face again.

Maybe it was a good thing that he'd had so much prac-tice in turning devastation inwards. Shutting it behind barriers that were impregnable. At least, they had been until Emma had come into his life.

Well… Adam turned on his heel and walked away. He'd just have to do a better job of building them this time, wouldn't he?

CHAPTER TEN

SOMETHING WAS WRONG.

Emma walked into the reception area of the Braeburn medical centre with a smile on her face because she'd been thinking about the first time she'd come through these doors and how different it felt now. Back then, she'd faced the snappy little terrier of a woman whom she'd thought was the children's grandmother and she'd been nervous of the fiercely uncompromising—almost angry—first impression of her potential employer.

Now she knew that Eileen was a loyal receptionist and that, behind the shield, Adam was a passionate and caring man. The most wonderful man she would ever meet in her life.

But her smile vanished as soon as she stepped through the door.

Caitlin had texted her to say that the children would be waiting at the clinic to be collected when she got back and Emma had assumed that Adam was too busy to take them home. Sure enough, the waiting room was packed and Oliver and Poppy were sitting in the corner, but Emma still knew that something was wrong.

There was a basket of toys in the corner but the twins were simply sitting there very quietly, looking as though they were in some kind of trouble.

Nobody else was talking either. Three women, one of whom she recognised as Moira, the Braeburn choir mistress, were intent on their knitting. Another rocked a pram that clearly contained a sleeping infant. Two men were invisible behind open newspapers.

Emma swallowed hard. She smiled at Eileen. 'I've just come to collect the children,' she said.

'Och, aye…' Eileen sniffed. 'We've been expecting you.'

Was that the problem? Was she later than she'd said she'd be? The coffee with Jack had turned into lunch but he'd been so kind and she'd needed someone to talk to. Somehow it made the new joy in her life more real to talk about it but it had the downside of making her fears a lot bigger as well. She'd ended up crying but Jack had held her hand and listened. He'd focused on the good re-sults of the first blood tests that had come through and reminded her of how well they'd predicted results of the bone-marrow tests in the past.

But she'd said she'd be back by three p.m. and it was only a little later than that because it had started snow-ing again and the train journey had been slow. She'd gone to where the car was parked, too, to hide all her parcels so that the children wouldn't guess she'd been shopping for them.

'How was the rehearsal?' Emma pasted another smile onto her face. 'I'm so sorry I missed it. You'll have to tell me all about it on the way home.'

Oliver was staring at his hands. Poppy's bottom lip wobbled as she looked up at Emma.

'Daddy's cross,' she whispered.

'Is he? Well…he's awfully busy.' Emma glanced around the waiting room. Of course Adam would be an-noyed that she hadn't been here to look after his children so he could do his job. That was what she'd been employed for, wasn't it? Except she was more than an employee now, wasn't she?

A prickle ran down Emma's spine. There was more to this than inconvenience. There was something heavy in the air. Something dark. Had somebody died maybe?

The door to the consulting room flew open and someone wrapped in a heavy coat bustled out. There was a short silence and then Adam appeared in their wake.

'*Next*,' he barked.

'That's you, Moira,' Eileen said in a stage whisper.

The choir mistress got hurriedly to her feet, clutching her knitting, but the ball of wool escaped and rolled an impressively long way across the floor. She bent to pick it up but the wool caught on the buckle of her shoe.

'Sorry, Doctor.' She tugged at the wool. A knitting needle came loose and clattered to the floor but Adam wasn't watching the progress of his next patient. His gaze had found Emma standing beside the children.

Suddenly it wasn't amusing to remember the first time she'd been here. Before Adam had known anything about her and had looked at her with a level of suspicion that had suggested she was the last person who might be suitable for looking after his precious children.

That kind of look paled in comparison to the chilly determination with which he was regarding her now. There was no suspicion in this glare. No doubt. No hint of warmth either.

'Take your time, Moira,' he snapped. 'Emma—could I have a word, please? It'll only take a minute.'

The last words were directed at the waiting room in general as Adam turned back to his consulting room. Or perhaps they had been intended to mollify Eileen. If so, it hadn't worked. Moira clicked her tongue and shook her head, the wool snapping as she gave it a harder tug. Eileen's eyes narrowed as she appeared to put two and two together and realise that Emma was somehow responsible for the doctor's bad mood.

This wasn't fair. Okay, she'd been absent for a little over twenty-four hours but it was hardly the crime of the century, was it? It certainly wasn't fair to make the children suffer and she'd never seen the twins look so miserable.

And her painkillers had worn off. A deep ache in her hip made it almost impossible to walk without a limp but somehow she managed it, knowing how many sets of eyes were watching every move she made.

'Shut the door, please,' Adam said, as she went in. 'Have a seat.'

'I'm...okay.' It was better to remain standing. Getting up from a chair might be painful enough to be difficult to hide.

'As you wish.'

He could have been speaking to a total stranger.

No. It was worse than that. He sounded as though he hated her and you couldn't hate someone you didn't know, could you? Emma couldn't stand this a moment longer.

'What's wrong, Adam? What have I done to upset you?'

A soft snort of unamused laughter came from Adam, accompanied by a head shake that emphasised his incredulity.

'I'm sorry if it's been difficult. Was there a problem with the children while I wasn't here or something?'

He was staring at her and, just for a heartbeat, Emma saw the barrier slip. If she'd thought the children looked miserable, it was nothing compared to the pain she saw in that instant in Adam's eyes. He looked...*betrayed*.

'I *know* why you had to go to Edinburgh,' he said.

'What?' Emma could actually feel the blood draining from her face.

'I took a patient through to the infirmary this morning.' Adam's eyes didn't leave hers. His tone was deceptively calm.

Dangerous.

'I *saw* you.'

Oh…dear Lord… He *did* know why she'd been there. He was a doctor who was well known at that hospital. How hard would it have been to get someone to check records and find out what she'd been even so briefly admitted for?

'I…I'm sorry, Adam. I should have told you the truth.'

'Just what the hell did you think you were playing at, Emma? Did you give any thought at all to how this was going to play out down the track? How it might affect the children? *Me*?'

When she *died*? Oh…help. She was going to cry. All she had wanted to do was offer her love.

To be loved in return, for just a blink of time. To make her last Christmas the best one ever.

How selfish had she been?

But the stunning effect of Adam's discovery was wearing off and guilt was getting overtaken by something else. Hurt. How cruel was this to be reminding her that she might not have much time left? To suggest that the effect on the McAllister family was worse than what she might have to face herself?

And why were the children looking so upset?

Emma's inward breath was almost a gasp. 'Have you told Ollie and Poppy?'

'No.' The word was a snap. 'And I don't want to.'

Thank goodness for that. The children must have simply picked up on the atmosphere and then assumed—as children were so good at doing—that it was somehow *their* fault. That was cruel, too, if it wasn't fixed. Emma would fix it as soon as she could.

'What I *do* want,' Adam continued, 'is for you to leave Braeburn. As soon as possible. I realise that it may be too late today but there should be trains running tomorrow. I've booked a room at The Inn for you. That's nice and close to the station.'

'But tomorrow's Christmas Eve.'

'I'm aware of the date.'

'I'm supposed to be helping with the school concert. The…the children's nativity play.'

'You can make some excuse. A family emergency perhaps.'

'And just…leave? Walk out and leave everybody to fill in the gap?'

'We managed before you came, Emma.' Adam was shuffling some papers on his desk now. 'We'll manage after you go.'

He expected her to go now, didn't he? To leave his office and then go home to pack and leave his house. She was being dismissed from her position as a nanny. From her position as his lover. Did he really have no intention of even *talking* about that?

Okay. She could understand why the barriers had gone back up. He knew she had made an offer of something she might not be able to follow through on and he'd seen history repeating itself with a loss in the near future that would have a dreadful effect on the children. And on himself? That was bitter-sweet. He was telling her how much she meant to him even as he pushed her away.

Maybe if it wasn't Christmastime, this wouldn't be happening like this. She'd been the one to force the celebration back into Adam's life and now it must seem like she was about to break his heart in exactly the same way it had been broken three years ago, when he'd lost the love of his life and his children had lost their beloved mother.

This was the first Christmas the children would be really celebrating at home and they were so excited about the play. About being the key characters of Joseph and Mary and—even more—about Jemima being part of the production. It had been her idea to include Jemima. Would that even happen if she wasn't here?

That did it. This might be all her fault but she wasn't going to let everything be ruined.

'No,' she said.

Adam looked up from his papers. 'I beg your pardon?'

'No,' Emma repeated. 'I understand why you want me to go…' Her voice wobbled. She couldn't say anything about how upset she was at him ending what they'd had between them like this because if she went down that track, she'd lose all the courage she knew she needed. 'But I'm not going to leave while I'm needed here. I can find somewhere else to stay but I promised Caitlin I'd be there to help with the singing and the play and…and I promised the children I'd be there.' She lifted her chin and took a steadying breath so that she could sound totally in control. 'I never break my promises.'

Caitlin would put her up for a night or two. Or she could stay at The Inn if that wasn't possible. She'd just have to dream up some reason for her absence to keep Poppy and Oliver as happy as possible.

Adam was looking at his papers again. 'Do what you need to,' he growled. 'I'll cope.'

Where had she heard those words before? Emma wondered, as she managed to find a smile for Oliver and Poppy as she led them out of the clinic.

Oh, yes… That had been exactly what Adam had said when she'd asked for the time off to go to Edinburgh. When she'd lied to him about the job interview.

'Is Daddy still cross?' Poppy asked as Emma clipped the belt over her car seat.

'No, sweetheart. And he was never cross with you.'

'Who was he cross with, then?' Oliver asked.

Me, Emma thought. And she had brought it on herself with her deception. She took another one of those steadying breaths.

'Sometimes grown-ups get cross because there's too much to do and people need things that are hard to give them. Daddy has to help lots of people and sometimes it's hard. Like when Mrs Jessop's baby was so sick.'

'But you help lots of people, too, and *you* don't get cross.'

Emma leaned in to kiss Poppy before she closed the door. In the time it took her to get to the driver's seat, inspiration had struck.

'Miss McMurray has an awful lot to do at the moment to get ready for your concert tomorrow. I know she doesn't get cross very often but I'm going to go and help her to make sure she doesn't. It might get very late so I'll probably stay at her house.'

'But you'll come back, won't you?' Poppy sounded anxious. 'It's only *two* sleeps till Christmas.'

'It *is*.' Emma turned on the car's lights and the windscreen wipers. 'Oh…look at how hard it's snowing. Isn't that pretty?'

Adam's parting words replayed themselves like an echo in Emma's head as she went through what had become such a joyous routine of caring for children and pets and trying to cook. She was getting better at it but it was a bonus to find one of Catherine's casseroles hiding in the freezer when she went to find some frozen peas. It had been wedged behind the turkey.

What had Catherine said about that? Didn't it need to come out of the freezer two days before Christmas so that it had time to thaw? Emma lifted the heavy bird and put it in the scullery tub. Not that she'd be here to cook it and maybe that was for the best. There was no way Adam could avoid celebrating Christmas now, what with all the decorations all over the house and the tree there waiting for the gifts to appear. At least she'd given this little family that much. And Adam probably knew how to cook a turkey.

As he'd said, he'd cope.

The first time he'd said those words had been the turning point, hadn't it? When Emma had decided that the real gift she could give Adam was hope. To show him what it could be like to let someone close. To be really happy again.

Well, it had worked, hadn't it?

Too well.

He'd accepted that gift and given his own in return. He'd shown her what it was like to be truly loved.

And now he knew that it had been false hope that she had offered.

But how could he be so sure? Did he know something that she didn't know? Emma stood there in the scullery, staring at the frozen turkey without seeing it. Had accessing her medical records somehow given him information that Jack had been unwilling to give her so close to Christmas?

A lightning bolt unleashed itself from the dark cloud that was pressing ever closer. If only she hadn't agreed to have the test so soon she could have kept it at bay for just a little longer.

There was no way to push it back now. All she could do was honour the promises she had made and then find somewhere she could gather strength to deal with the storm when it finally broke.

California maybe?

She was gone.

This time, the silence of the house had an almost ominous edge. It wasn't just an overnight absence. Emma was gone from his house and after tomorrow she would be gone from his life as well.

Adam had been late home after going to check that Jock was coping back on the farm and the children were already tucked up in bed and asleep. Emma's bag had been sitting beside her guitar case near the clock and within minutes of his arrival Caitlin McMurray had driven up to collect her. His dinner was keeping warm in the stove, she'd told him. The turkey was thawing in the scullery tub and she'd left some gifts under the Christmas tree and hoped that would be okay. And she'd said that she was sorry…so very sorry…

Too weary to feel hungry, Adam sat on a chair at the kitchen table beneath all those rainbow-coloured paper chains and downed the last shot his whisky bottle had to offer. The emotional roller-coaster of his day had left him drained enough to feel numb.

Or maybe not completely numb. There was pain to be found that had to be coming from the broken shards of that glass bubble of hope. And pain was a close neighbour to anger. Easy to step over the boundary and preferable to direct the anger towards someone else. He'd used this method of defence before but he knew it came with some fine print. It was only a matter of time before the anger turned inwards and became a sense of failure. He hadn't been enough as a husband.

He hadn't even been enough as a lover this time around.

Was he enough as a doctor? Joan McClintock probably thought so by now, as she lay in the cardiology ward of the infirmary, recovering from her angioplasty. And Old Jock definitely did. He'd said as much when Adam had taken the groceries that Eileen had put together and gone up the hill to visit him. He could swear there had been tears in the old man's eyes when Jock had gripped his arm in farewell.

'You and that wee lassie saved my life, son. I might not be up to playing my pipes tomorrow but I'll be back on deck next year, you wait and see.'

The Jessops would be spending a quiet Christmas in the neonatal intensive care unit but it would be a celebration because they'd be able to hold their precious new baby and talk about the day in the not-too-distant future when they'd be able to take her home. She'd need careful monitoring for her first years of life but it would be a joy to be responsible for that.

Yes. Adam could take comfort in knowing that he *was* enough of a doctor for this village. That he was deeply woven into the community fabric and he was needed here.

Was he enough as a father?

With a heavy tread and two unusually subdued dogs, Adam climbed the staircase of his old family home and went to check on his sleeping children. Oliver lay sprawled on his back at an angle that had his head almost touching the wheels of the train engine tucked in the corner beside his pillow. Adam gently moved the toy as he bent to kiss his son.

Poppy was rolled into a ball and her eyes were squeezed tightly shut. She had her Gran's old teddy clutched in her arms.

'Are you awake, sweetheart?' Adam whispered.

She must be dreaming, he decided when he got no response. He pulled the duvet up to cover her back and kissed the top of her head.

'Sleep tight,' he murmured. 'Love you.'

The hallway outside the children's rooms was quiet and still. The half-open door of the empty guest room further down was eloquent enough to be an accusation. There would be no music coming from that room again. No small, fairy-like woman would emerge with joy in her eyes and laughter just waiting to bubble free. With hands and lips and a body that could make a man feel like…like he was, well, more than enough.

Maybe it would help to shut the door.

Adam wasn't sure why he flicked the light on. Perhaps because it seemed suddenly beyond belief that Emma *had* really gone?

The room was empty, of course. The bed neatly made. A vase that his mother must have put in here before she'd left had a sprig of holly in it—a fragment of the festive bowl that was on the kitchen table downstairs. A tiny bit of the Christmas Emma had been so determined to spread throughout this house.

And there was something else. A glint under the bed that the light was catching. Stooping, Adam found it was a disk. A copy of the recording made with Braeburn school's junior choir? He'd heard all about it but he hadn't actually heard the singing, had he? And it wasn't good enough. With the disk in his hand Adam went back downstairs and into the library to turn on the computer. The fire was only a glow in the grate but the dogs curled up as close as they could on the rug.

He had expected to only hear sound when he pushed play on the menu. The image that filled the screen was a shock. It was Emma and another young woman. The photo must have been taken with a mobile phone. Two happy girls at a party somewhere. Emma looked so much younger. Her hair was a thick mass of curls and her face was different. Plumper. Carefree.

He should have stopped right there—the moment he knew that this was something personal and nothing to do with his children or their carol singing—but the photo was dissolving into the next image in the slide show and the exquisite plucked notes of the guitar were being accompanied by words.

It was the song he'd come to know from the snatches he'd heard late at night as he'd paused at the top of the stairs. A song about memories and friendship. About love. He knew he was seeing something never intended for his eyes when he recognised the man that he'd seen Emma with at the hospital today and he would have stopped it except that the next image was so shocking.

Emma in a hospital bed, completely bald and with her face unnaturally puffy. An IV line snaked beneath the hem of her gown.

Of course. He'd been right in thinking what that tiny scar was about. She'd had a central line inserted as a portal for major drug therapy.

Chemotherapy. That was the only thing that could make someone look like this. And you only got chemotherapy for cancer treatment.

And yet Emma was smiling. Laughing, even? It was so easy to recognise her despite the drastically altered

appearance because the image captured that joy that was
what Emma was all about.

The stunning effect was still there even as the image
dissolved into a new one and it was only then that Adam
could register the words of the song's chorus.

*We've shared the sunshine and we've shared the
rain...*
Just by being there, you eased the pain...

He couldn't see the next image. Or the next, because
his vision had blurred. He barely heard the rest of the
song as he bent his head and covered his eyes with his
hands.

The longing was too much.

He wanted to be the one to share the good times with
Emma. To be there to hold her in the bad times.

Was she still sick? Was *that* why she'd been at the infirmary?

The longing morphed into a fierce protectiveness. A
need to care for her for as long as possible—even if they
both knew it might not be very long.

Maybe there was another man who was special to
her and there was no future for *him* with Emma, but she
might know that she didn't have much time left and she'd
chosen to be *here*. Not with anyone else but with him
and his children. To give herself in every way possible
to make this Christmas special. It was only now that it
was dawning on him how incredibly lucky they'd been.

The children were going to be heartbroken to wake
up on Christmas morning to a house that contained the
gifts but not the person who'd chosen them. The magic
she'd created would be spoilt.

And he'd been the one to send her away. She would

be leaving Braeburn as soon as tomorrow's concert was over. He'd never have the chance to tell her what she'd given his children in making Christmas happen. What she'd given him in that he now knew he was capable of letting go of the past and that he could find real joy in his life again.

That he could feel hope.

A nudge under his elbow made Adam uncover his eyes. He hadn't noticed the dogs coming to flank his chair and the steady gaze from Bob offered limitless sympathy and something more. Wisdom? He scratched his old dog's ears.

'You're right,' he murmured. 'I can't let that happen, can I?'

CHAPTER ELEVEN

'JANET CALLED WHILE you were in the shower.'

'Oh?' Emma sipped the mug of coffee Caitlin had put in front of her. 'Who's Janet?'

'My brother's girlfriend's aunt. The one who runs the donkey sanctuary.'

'Oh…is there a problem? I thought she was delighted to help with getting Jemima to the concert. Is it the snow?' Emma took a worried glance out of the window. 'It is getting awfully heavy, isn't it?'

Caitlin laughed. 'Don't stress. I'm doing that enough for both of us. No. Aunty Janet's still as keen as mustard. In fact, she's bringing an extra donkey. He's called Dougal.'

'But we don't need *two* donkeys.'

'He's back-up—just in case Jemima doesn't want to co-operate. Apparently Dougal's done this sort of thing before. He's a darling, Janet says, and if Jemima's not used to getting into a float then having another donkey can help. Plus…'

Emma had to smile at Caitlin's expression and the raised forefinger that advertised how important this was. The connection she'd found with this new friend was partly due to how their imaginations were caught by the same things. She had to try and squash the sadness of how much she was going to miss this friendship. Caitlin hadn't asked about how soon she would be leaving Braeburn. She only knew that she was no longer needed as the McAllister nanny.

'Plus what?'

'Well... Dougal's looking for a new home. Janet was a bit worried when she heard that Jemima is an only donkey. She says they get very lonely by themselves and they can get very noisy.'

'Jemima's certainly noisy.' Poppy had said the same thing, hadn't she? That Jemima needed a friend. Another wave of sadness hit as she remembered the time with the children that day. When they'd picked the bunch of holly and made the paper chains. She was so going to miss their laughter and cuddles and the sheer joy of singing together.

'So what I'm saying is that Dougal doesn't necessarily have to go back to the sanctuary. He could be a Christmas gift for the McAllister family.'

'Oh...that's a lovely idea...but...' Emma bit her lip. It wasn't her place to accept, was it? She'd already given things to the McAllisters that were going to have long-term consequences. The thought of the damage she might have done had already formed a horrible knot in her stomach. 'You'll have to ask Adam about that.'

'I'll get Janet to talk to him. She's very persuasive.' With a nod and another smile Caitlin moved on to the next item on the agenda for her busy day. 'I need to talk to Moira about finding another piper to open the concert. Old Jock's always done it but he's not well enough this time. I don't want to offend him by asking someone whose playing he doesn't respect, though.'

Emma grinned. 'Village politics, huh?'

'You're not wrong there.' But Caitlin looked up from

her list, shaking her head. 'You know, it usually takes a generation or more before someone becomes part of the heart of a village like this. You've managed to do it in the space of a few weeks.'

'Hardly. I'm still a stranger.' But Emma had to swallow a big lump in her throat. She *felt* like a part of the heart of Braeburn, which was something that could only have happened so fast because it felt like the place she was supposed to be. With the people she was supposed to be with.

'You saved Jock,' Caitlin reminded her. 'You've saved the village hall with the funds that CD's going to raise. Plus...' She held up her finger again. 'You've saved my reputation as the teacher who can pull the end-of-the-year concert together.' She heaved a huge sigh. 'There are still a million things to do, though. There's the backdrop to paint and the hall to decorate and hay to get delivered and I don't know if Bryan's finished making the cradle yet. And I've got to ring Jeannie's mum to make sure they don't forget to bring the baby doll and...'

Emma finished her coffee. This was good. She would be too busy to dwell on what would happen after the concert. 'What can I do to help?'

'Ye canna say no.'

'But, Jock...I haven't touched the pipes in years.' The Velcro of the blood-pressure cuff made a decisive ripping sound as Adam removed it from Old Jock's arm. 'I'd be as rusty as your coronary arteries were before the stents went in.'

'Nonsense, lad.' The old man fixed Adam with a steely glance. 'No laddie I taught ever forgets and you were the best. There's no one else I'd choose to take my place and

I told that McMurray lassie from the school that I'd find my own replacement.'

He didn't have time to stand here arguing with Jock. It had taken time to organise the children this morning and get them to their friends' houses for the day so that he could check on his patients and be available for any emergencies. They'd been so slow, too. Uncooperative. Oliver had kicked his chair more than once and refused to even look for his songbook and Poppy had been in tears and refused to eat any breakfast.

'I want Emma to make my breakfast,' she'd sobbed. 'I *love* Emma.'

He had to try and be home at four p.m. as well for the woman who was coming to collect Jemima in a float. Emma should be there for that, shouldn't she? It had been her crazy idea in the first place. But it was his fault that she wouldn't be there and he had to start fixing his mistake somewhere.

But to wear his kilt… To pick up his beloved pipes that had been gathering dust for three years or more…

Emma would be there.

He wouldn't just be playing for the village and showing them that he was ready to embrace life fully again.

He would be playing for Emma. Showing her the man he really was—the man he wanted to be again. He'd heard so much of her music but she'd never heard his.

Could it be a way to connect again? A chance to talk?

Maybe even a way to persuade her to come back to where she was needed so much?

To come back home?

'All right, then.' The words were the kind of growl everyone was used to from Dr Adam McAllister. 'I'll do it. What song did you have in mind?'

'The usual.' Jock's nod was satisfied. There was even a hint of a smile on the craggy face. '"O Come All Ye Faithful".'

The stars didn't align well enough for him to make it home by four p.m. and see Jemima loaded into the float, but the donkey was missing so presumably they'd managed without him. At least now he had the time to go and let the dogs out and to collect his bagpipes.

He wasn't the only person who'd been out and about, doing his job, today. A courier had been to the farmhouse and left a special-delivery letter. Unfortunately, he hadn't chosen a good place to leave it and enough snow or sleet had landed to make it very soggy. Soggy enough for the envelope to disintegrate as he picked it up.

It was addressed to Emma, not him, so he had no right to look at its contents.

And he wouldn't have, except that he could see that the stationery was stamped with the logo of the infirmary and he thought that there had to be some mistake and that the letter *should* have been addressed to him.

They were blood-test results. A whole raft of them. With a sticky note stuck to the top one.

Proof. Couldn't be better so far, Em.
Happy Christmas, love, Jack.

Jack. The man in the photograph. The man at the hospital. The 'almost' brother who had become a specialist oncologist and had looked after Emma's mother.

Who was clearly looking after Emma now. His signature was on the test results. This *was* why she'd been at the hospital.

His head was spinning.

He'd known, at some level, how wrong it was to assume that Emma was deceiving him in the same way Tania had so often.

But why had she looked so stricken when he'd told her he knew why she was there? So *guilty*?

Because she'd been less than forthcoming about the nature of her 'appointment'?

Oh…dear Lord…did she think he was rejecting her because she was sick?

He *had* to talk to her as soon as possible. Never mind thanking her for what she'd done for the children or for him. He had the biggest apology in his life to make.

But he had a duty to do as well. He couldn't break his promise to Jock.

He had to find those pipes. And he had to get dressed for the part. A small part, thank goodness. He'd find a way to talk to Emma as soon as it was over.

The snow had stopped falling over Braeburn village on the night before Christmas. The cobbles of the narrow streets were sleek and dark where they'd been swept clear hours before but the perfect, white snow lay in a soft blanket on rooftops and gardens. It covered the bench where Emma had sat so many times to listen to Jock play his bagpipes and it coated the branches of the huge Christmas tree in the square, which only made the lights seem to twinkle even more brightly.

Not that there was anybody to appreciate the pretty picture. Most of Braeburn's inhabitants seemed to have squeezed themselves somehow into the village hall so that there wasn't even standing room any more.

Peeping through the curtains that were keeping several dozen excited children and just as many adult support crew hidden, Emma still couldn't see Adam anywhere.

Surely he wasn't going to miss seeing his children perform? Her frown deepened as she noticed the size of the gap visible in the crowded space that led in a straight line from the entrance to the stage. Would Jemima really cope with carrying Poppy down that narrow aisle?

Aunty Janet didn't seem to think they'd have any problem.

'She's a darling,' she'd informed Emma that afternoon. 'Went onto the float without any trouble at all and then she fell in love with Dougal on the spot. She'll be perfectly happy until it's her turn to perform.'

Which wouldn't be for a little while, although the concert was about to start. The main lights had been dimmed so that only the fairy-lights they'd hung on the walls were twinkling now, lighting up the spruce boughs and holly branches. An expectant silence grew until it felt like the audience was holding its breath, and then Emma heard a familiar sound—somewhere between a honk and a screech—that would have had Sharon putting her fingers in her ears, no doubt. Someone, out in the foyer, was warming up a set of bagpipes. Caitlin hadn't told her who she'd found that could replace Jock without causing offence, but as the first true notes sounded it was obvious that a good choice had been made.

Who knew that bagpipes could play a Christmas carol with such haunting beauty? Coming down the aisle, it was too dark to see the face of the man holding the pipes but he was pure Scot, with the folds of a kilt brushing bare knees and long socks as white as the snow outside. The sight and sound would have been stirring no matter what was being played but the Christmas carol gave it an extra depth that brought tears to Emma's eyes.

This was about Scotland—the place she'd fallen in

love with—and about such a special time of year that was all about celebration and family.

And there was a family she'd fallen even more in love with here.

As the lone piper came closer, Emma was sure it was her imagination—or the tears misting her vision—that made her think it was Adam playing the bagpipes. But right in front of the stage he stopped and lowered the pipes before turning to exit from the side door, and there was no mistaking his identity.

He was her gorgeous, gentle Scotsman. The lonely man whose heart she had touched—and then broken again.

She could feel a piece of her own heart being torn off in that moment.

Never again would she love someone as much as she loved this man.

Would it make any difference if she told him about the conversation she'd had with Jack this morning? That the initial results of all her blood tests were so good that he was confident she'd beaten her disease and could look forward to a normal life? He'd known how hard it was for her to believe. He'd said he was sending a copy of the results for her by courier.

It was the Christmas gift she'd wanted above anything else. It should have made her feel ecstatic and yet here she was, watching Adam exit the crowded hall to loud applause, and she was having to fight back tears.

The fear that she had lost something that would have made every moment of the battle she'd had to keep her life more than worthwhile.

Not that there was any time for that dark thought to last more than a heartbeat. The curtains were being drawn back now. Poppy needed a kiss and words of encouragement as she joined the other tiny dancers to start the evening's proceedings.

'You look gorgeous, hon,' Emma whispered. 'I just love that new kilt that Daddy got for you. He's going to be *so* proud of you.'

She had expected Poppy to be bouncing up and down with excitement and that she would have to say how much she *loved* kilts. Or dancing. Or Christmas. But the little girl seemed uncharacteristically solemn and she clung so tightly to Emma's neck that she had to prise the little arms free as the dance teacher clapped her hands to shoo the troupe of girls into position.

It was Oliver's turn to perform with the other boys on the chanters next but Emma couldn't stop to watch. She had to get Poppy changed into her blue dress and shawl to be Mary amidst the chaos of mothers putting the final touches of moustaches and beards onto the wise men and shepherds and Caitlin trying to be in five places at once as last-minute adjustments were made to the nativity set behind the second curtain. The mothers would take care of Oliver's costume during the next item, which was an older girl reciting a Christmas poem. Emma's job was to go outside and help Janet get Jemima into position and primed for the grand entry.

The icy night air found the gap between Adam's socks and the hem of his kilt and made him shiver as he slipped outside during the applause for his son's performance. Behind him, he could hear Maggie MacEwen being introduced and then the girl's clear voice as she began her recital.

'"'Twas the night before Christmas, when all through the house…not a creature was stirring, not even a mouse…"'

Rounding the side of the village hall, Adam could see where the float was parked. He knew that Emma would have to bring the children and Jemima down this path so that they could make their entrance to the hall.

It still seemed unbelievable that his family's pet donkey was about to star in the traditional nativity play for the village. As extraordinary as the person who'd made it happen?

Yes.

Once she had Oliver and Poppy and Jemima into position at the front entrance of the hall, Adam knew she would take her position on the stage as the curtains were drawn back. With the music from her guitar and her lovely voice, she would lead the junior choir in singing the 'Little Donkey' carol for what would be a breathtaking opening for the traditional play that was the finale of the Christmas concert. Adam couldn't wait to see it.

But he didn't want it to start just yet. Not until he'd had a chance to talk to Emma.

Seeing her slight figure beside the float, holding the lead rope attached to Jemima's halter, made Adam's heart squeeze so tightly it felt like it might burst. She'd won the hearts of so many of those people tucked into the warmth of the old hall beside them, including his own children.

Especially including him.

He hadn't known it was possible to fall in love so fast—and so completely—with someone. Emma had not only won his heart, she would have it for ever, whether she wanted it or not.

She probably didn't want it. Not after the way he'd treated her. But he had to at least tell her how he felt. To explain why he'd reacted the way he had. To take the risk of making himself completely vulnerable in order to fight for the woman he loved so much.

'Emma…'

'Adam…' Emma looked startled but then relieved. 'Can you persuade Jemima to move? Ollie's still getting changed and she won't budge for me.'

Adam took hold of the donkey's halter and made encouraging noises but it was like trying to move a very large rock.

'She's no' going anywhere,' Janet—the woman who'd collected Jemima that afternoon—said. 'No' without Dougal. She's fallen in love.'

'What?' Adam peered inside the float to where he could see the fluffy back end of another donkey. 'There's another donkey?'

'Aye…' Janet's stare seemed intense in the soft light from the hall windows. 'I brought him in case she didn't like the idea of going in the float. But it seems that she's a very lonely donkey. She needs love in her life.'

'Don't we all?' Adam turned to Emma, who was also staring at him with a curious expression. One of hope? Janet had disappeared into the float. 'Emma, I need to talk to you. I—'

'Dougal needs a home.' The donkey had followed her down the ramp. 'Jemima doesn't need to be lonely any more.'

As if to add her opinion, Jemima made a soft, whickering sound and pulled away from Emma to touch her nose to Dougal's. The two donkeys stood there, side by side, their bodies pressed together.

'Do you think you could?' Yes. It was definitely hope in Emma's eyes. 'Adopt Dougal?'

Adam wanted to see her smile. To see the joy he knew would appear, even if it had nothing to do with him.

'Aye… If Jemima's in love then it wouldn't be right to separate them, would it?'

'No...' Emma was smiling. 'And it would make Poppy so happy if Jemima had a friend.' There was more than joy in her eyes. They were soft and full of love. Was it too much to hope that some of that love might include him?

Adam took a deep breath but just as he opened his mouth a figure came swiftly towards them from the street.

'Dr McAllister—thank goodness I've found you. You have to come—quickly. Bryan's fallen off his ladder. He was trying to fix the lights outside The Inn and he's come a cropper. I think he might have killed himself...'

For just a heartbeat longer Adam held Emma's gaze but there was nothing he could say. Not yet. All he could do was to try and communicate that this conversation wasn't finished.

It hadn't even begun, in fact.

He turned away. 'I'm coming,' he said. 'Let me grab my bag.'

It took only a few minutes to get to the scene of the accident. Bryan had, indeed, come a cropper and had probably knocked himself out for a short time. He had a good-sized lump on his head and had a mild concussion, but there didn't seem to be anything seriously amiss. But by the time they'd got him inside to the warmth and Adam had given him a thorough check, repeating his neurological checks at five-minute intervals, and finally decided it wasn't necessary to call an ambulance, at least half an hour had passed.

By the time he got back to the village hall, he knew he had probably missed everything. The entrance of the children, with Poppy riding Jemima, the singing of the children, the whole play perhaps. At least it was being videoed but the twins would be so disappointed that he hadn't been there. He searched for them on the stage where every performer had gathered for a final carol but he couldn't see them.

Emma wasn't there with her guitar either.

And where was Caitlin? Was there a problem backstage?

The children gathered on the stage were getting restless. A hum of conversation began in the audience, too. It was getting later and a new snowfall could start at any moment. Everybody was ready to go home.

Adam ducked back out the front door and raced around to the side entrance near the stage. He almost knocked someone over who was rushing in the opposite direction.

'Adam... *Oh...*' Emma sounded distraught. 'Have you seen the twins?'

'No. They're not on the stage with the other children.'

'They're not anywhere...' Emma's breath came out in a sob. 'They've *disappeared*...'

Janet and Caitlin weren't far behind Emma. 'The donkeys are gone too. I had them in the float. I was just looking for someone to help me lift the back door.'

'Jemima must have undone the knots.' Emma's voice was shaking. Oliver had told her how clever she was at doing that, hadn't he? 'The children must have gone looking for them...'

Caitlin put her arm around Emma's shoulders but she was looking at Adam. 'They can't have gone far, surely?'

'But it's so dark...' Emma whispered. 'And cold...'

Adam had had plenty of practice in his career of not allowing panic to gain a foothold but this was the hardest test ever.

'It's been snowing,' he said, struggling to keep his tone calm. 'The tracks will be easy to follow. We'll get a group to follow where the donkeys have gone and others to look for what direction the children have gone, just in case they're not together.'

The snow was falling more thickly now. Silent, fluffy, fat flakes that would quickly obliterate any tracks.

They were already running out of time.

'Caitlin—go inside and round up as many people as you can to help us look. Make sure they've got at least one person with a mobile phone in each group. Janet—go with someone who'll help you follow the donkeys' tracks. You'll be the best person to manage them. Emma?'

Her gaze locked with his instantly.

'Come with me.' Her hand joined his outstretched one just as quickly. He held her gaze for a heartbeat longer but he didn't need to say anything.

They both knew they had to find the children. Nothing else mattered.

CHAPTER TWELVE

THE CALL TO action was taken up by every able-bodied adult present in the village hall on that Christmas Eve.

The children were kept in the warmth, guarded by Caitlin and a group of mothers. Braeburn's policeman, Angus, organised everybody else into groups that fanned out from the hall to cover every possible direction the children might have taken.

By the time the groups began moving, Adam and Emma were already in the village square. The lights on the big tree and in the shop windows twinkled as merrily as ever but the square was deserted and Adam's groan of frustration a loud sound in the kind of silence that only came in a snow-covered landscape.

'I thought they'd be here. They could never get enough of coming to see the tree in the last couple of years.'

Having her own hope snatched away had left too much room for fear to fill. Emma's gaze raked the area she knew so well now but there was no sign of any small people and the snow was a smooth carpet. The only footprints to be seen were the ones they were making themselves.

'But it hasn't been like that this year.' Adam seemed to be thinking aloud. 'Because they've got a Christmas tree at home, haven't they?' He raised his voice. '*Ollie*? *Poppy*? Can you hear me? Where *are* you?'

In the distance, they could hear others calling the children's names. Much closer came another shout as a square of light appeared between the windows of the local pub.

'What's going on? Is that you, Doc?'

'Aye, Bryan.' Adam walked towards the inn keeper. 'The twins have wandered off from the hall. We don't know where they are.'

'On a night like this? I'll get my coat and help you look.'

'No. You're supposed to be resting that head of yours. But if you see anything, call Angus. He's in charge of the search parties.'

'I will but I canna understand why the bairns would have done that.' Bryan shook his head as he stepped forward to grip Adam's arm. 'But they'll be all right. They've got an angel looking out for them, haven't they?'

'Aye…' But Adam had already turned away.

Why *had* the children run away? Emma's hand was on Adam's arm the moment Bryan let go.

'They must be looking for you,' she said. 'Maybe they realised you weren't there to see the play.'

'I *wanted* to be there.' The growl reminded Emma of when she'd first met Adam. 'I had no choice…'

'I know that. I'm not blaming you.' Emma squeezed his arm more tightly. 'But where would they go if they wanted to find you? The medical centre?'

'Aye… That's a thought.'

Adam started to move so swiftly that Emma slipped on the cobbles as she tried to keep up. This time it was Adam who caught her arm and then he took hold of her hand again and slowed his pace a little.

Please, be there, Emma prayed silently. *Be sitting on the steps of the clinic, waiting for your daddy.*

But they weren't. The steps were covered by inches of perfect white snow.

'Oh…*no*…' Emma whispered. 'I'm sorry, Adam. We've come the wrong way.'

'It's not your fault. It was a good idea.'

'It *is* my fault. I should have been watching them. It was my job and I didn't do it well enough.' The tear that trickled down felt hot against her frozen skin.

'If it's anybody's fault, it's mine,' Adam said. 'I sent you away. It was my responsibility to look after my children.' He hit his forehead with the palm of his hand. 'I didn't *think*…'

'You're the only doctor this village has. Of course you had to go when you were called to an accident. The children were safely in the hall with dozens of people.'

'I'm no' a good father. Just like I wasn't a good husband.'

'How can you *say* that?' Emma was shocked. 'You're a wonderful father. You love those children to bits, even if you've found it hard to show it sometimes. But everyone understands why. You had a perfect marriage. Everybody knows that your heart was broken when you lost the love of your life.'

'Nobody *knows*…' Adam was looking away from her. Poised to walk in the direction he was looking. To continue their urgent search.

'They do,' Emma insisted. '*I* know, too. And I'm sorry. I've only made things worse but I didn't mean to. I—'

'*She wasn't alone.*' The words were torn out of Adam. He still hadn't turned to meet Emma's gaze. 'When she died in that bed. Tania wasn't alone. She was with her lover. I wasn't enough of a husband for her.'

'*No...*' Shock was laced with anger this time as understanding sank in. As she realised that Adam had been living a lie for so long. To keep such an awful truth to himself to protect his children. Even his own mother didn't know because she'd never have spoken of Tania the way she had that first night if she did.

There was a complete lack of understanding mixed in as well. How could any woman have won the love of this beautiful man and then trampled on it with such devastating effect?

No wonder it was so hard for him to trust again. Or that he'd reacted to her own deception the way he had.

She had to get him to look at her so that he could see the truth. Reaching up, Emma touched his cheek, turning his head so that she could meet his eyes.

'*No*,' she repeated fiercely. '*She* wasn't a good enough wife for *you*.'

She could have come up with any number of reasons why Adam deserved to be truly loved but this wasn't the time and the interruption of Adam's phone ringing made Emma catch her breath. Good news? Had the children been found?

Adam's voice was loud a few moments later. 'What—no sign at all? What about the donkeys?'

He listened again. 'We'll have to go further than the village, then. It's stopped snowing now. If they're moving, they'll start leaving tracks again.'

If they were moving?

Emma couldn't bear to think of why they might not be moving.

Having snapped his phone shut, Adam stood very still and Emma knew he wasn't seeing the street. Or the square at the end where they could still see the flashes of the Christmas tree's lights.

'We need help,' he said slowly. 'A search and rescue team. Dogs.'

'Dogs…' The word was too quiet for Adam to hear. Maybe she hadn't even spoken it aloud but it was enough to trigger a powerful image. An old stone farmhouse at the end of a long drive, with a big kitchen and a fascinating attic. Fireplaces with dancing flames and snoozing dogs on the rugs.

Home.

The image morphed into something that felt like an absolute conviction.

'Adam? I know where they are.'

'Where?'

'They've gone home.'

'Why would they do that? It's miles away. They wouldn't make it. They're just wee bairns…'

'I just know it's the direction they will have taken. Let's get your car and check.'

'But how can you be so sure?'

'It's where I'd want to be,' Emma said softly. 'To be with you.'

For a long, long moment Adam held her gaze. Asking for something. Reassurance that the children would be found safe? Or maybe he was asking if *she* wanted to be with him?

All she could offer was hope.

And a hand to hold.

The house wasn't locked but as soon as they got out of the vehicle Adam knew there was no point in going inside, despite the urgent barking they could hear.

The driveway had been sheltered from a heavy cover of snow by the trees but the tracks were obvious in the headlights as soon as they got close to the house. Messy tracks that were more than just footprints that were marking a path that led towards the orchard and stables.

There was no time to find a torch so Adam used the light from his phone. He offered Emma his hand to guide her through the half-open gate and was still holding it when they got to the door of the stable.

It was a picture he would never forget as long as he lived.

Two donkeys curled up in the thick layer of straw, their noses touching. Between them, protected by the warmth of the fluffy bodies, were the two children. Oliver had one arm around Jemima's neck, his face pillowed on her neck. His other arm was around his sister. Poppy, in her blue dress, still had the baby doll clutched under her arm. Both the children had a healthy, rosy glow to their cheeks and were clearly deeply asleep. An exhausted Joseph and Mary with the baby. It was a nativity scene like no other.

The donkeys were awake. Four huge, dark eyes met the light but neither Jemima nor Dougal disturbed the children by even a twitch.

Adam's first instinct was to gather both children into his arms as if he would never let them go, and he would do that. But first there was something else he had to do. Quietly, he stepped back and made the call to Angus to relay the news that the children were safe and the search could be called off. The inhabitants of Braeburn village could go to their own homes and prepare to celebrate Christmas with their own families.

Emma was still close by and he turned to her as he ended the call. It was time to take the children in to their own beds but catching Emma's gaze stopped Adam again.

'I've been alone for a long time.' His voice caught. 'In a place that I never thought I could share with anyone.'

'I know.' She held his gaze. 'Thank you.'

'What for?'

'Trusting me.' She moved a little closer. 'I understand why you've kept the truth to yourself and that's something that will never go any further. The children—and the people of Braeburn—can always think that the mother of your children is an angel.'

'But you'll know…' Adam could hear the note of wonder in his own voice. 'And that means I'm not alone any more.' He had to swallow hard. 'It's me who should be thanking *you*.'

'There's no need.' It looked like Emma was trying to smile but he could see the way her lips trembled. He suddenly felt a little fragile himself.

'I found your song,' he told her. 'With the photographs. You left it behind yesterday. I'm sorry…I had no idea you were sick.'

'But you saw me at the hospital…'

'I got things wrong…' Adam closed his eyes. 'I saw you with Jack. Holding hands. I didn't know who he was and I thought…I'm sorry. It's no' been easy for me to learn to trust again.'

'But you trusted me tonight. You told me your terrible secret.'

'Aye…I already knew how wrong I'd been. Even before I knew who Jack was.' It was Adam's turn to move closer. Close enough to touch. To cup Emma's face and make sure she knew how much every word meant. 'I've been wrong about a lot of things but there's one thing I can never be wrong about. I love you. I want you to stay. With me. With the children. For as long as we've got.'

He saw a whole range of expressions flicker over the face of this woman he loved. Shock as she probably guessed what he'd thought when he'd seen her with

another man. Forgiveness as he admitted his error. The
birth of joy as he confessed his love.

And then she smiled.

'It might be a very long time. I haven't got the final
results of my bone-marrow test but so far everything's
looking as good as it possibly could.'

'It could never be long enough.' Adam put his arms
around Emma and drew her close. His kiss was slow and
tender. A promise of what he intended to show her properly, very soon.

'Let's get these bairns safely into their own beds.'

'Aye...' Emma's smile was one of pure joy. 'And then
we can get to ours?'

'Aye...'

With their arms still around each other, they went
back into the stable.

Poppy stirred as her father lifted her into his arms.
'Daddy...' Her eyes opened and she turned her head.
'*Emma*...you're back. You've come home.'

'I have, sweetheart.'

Oliver had woken up, too. 'I told you she wasn't going
away for ever,' he told his sister.

'But I saw you leave,' Poppy said. 'I saw you talking
to Daddy and you took your kit-ar and...and I was sad.'

'You don't need to be sad any more,' Adam said.
'Emma's not going anywhere.'

'You didn't see our play,' Oliver said. 'We went outside to find you and saw Jemima going home. We tried
to catch her and then we got lost.'

'She's got a friend now.' Poppy smiled at Emma. 'She's
got Dougal.'

'Dougal likes me,' Oliver said. 'He let me ride him and
Poppy rode Jemima and she took us home.'

'I was scared, Daddy.'

'So was I, poppet. So was I.'

'But everything's all right now.' Emma's eyes were bright with tears as she held out her hand to Oliver. 'Let's go inside and get you two into your nice warm beds.'

Poppy was almost asleep again in her father's arms.

'Emma came back,' she murmured. 'I *love* Emma.'

'So do I, pet.' Adam's whisper was loud enough for them all to hear. 'So do I.'

Emma, with Oliver's hand in hers, came close enough to lean against Adam's arm as she returned his tender smile. He could feel the connection of her body against his and he could see a far deeper connection in her eyes. Here they were—the four of them—all connected.

His family. And they were together. And safe. And very, very soon they would celebrate their first Christmas together. A new and wonderful joy misted his vision.

He knew that it would be the first of many, many Christmases.

EPILOGUE

A year later...

No CHRISTMAS COULD ever be as wonderful as this one.

Even the joy of being present for Holly's birth in Canada last year was completely outshone by this day, as far as Catherine McAllister was concerned.

They should have used the table in the big dining room to host a Christmas feast for so many people but the inhabitants of this house had been adamant that they wanted to eat in the kitchen. Like they always did.

Adam was at one end and his gorgeous wife of six months at the other. Darling Emma. Catherine had known as soon as she'd set eyes on the lass that magic was going to happen but she'd never have guessed at quite how much.

At the sides of the table it had been a fair squeeze to fit everybody in. Marion and Ian on one side, with baby Holly in her highchair beside her gran. On the other side was Emma's best friend Sharon, whom they'd all come to love when she'd come over from America to be the bridesmaid for a summer wedding in the Braeburn village church. This time she'd brought her husband Andy as well, and they were flanked by Poppy and Ollie.

There was so much laughter. Like when Adam had

been telling the story of how disastrous last year's Christmas dinner had been.

'Neither of us had any idea what to do with that turkey. It wasn't till after we took it out of the stove that we realised there was a plastic bag inside it.'

Sharon needed a pat on the back so that her amusement didn't choke her. 'I could have told you Emma didn't know how to cook,' she said finally.

'I'm learning,' Emma protested. 'I have the best mother-in-law in the world.'

The real truth was that Catherine was lucky enough to have the most amazing daughter-in-law in the world but she didn't say anything aloud. She just shared a fond glance with Emma and then smiled at how quickly Adam defended her.

'My wife has talents that are far more important than cooking.'

'What's a talent?' Oliver asked.

'It means you're really good at something. Like Emma is with playing her guitar and singing.'

Oliver's nod was solemn. 'Mummy's going to be famous, isn't she?'

'You bet she is, buddy.' Marion had come back from Canada with new expressions. 'I'm not surprised a record company's signed you. That song you wrote for Sharon is just beautiful. No, Holly, don't blow raspberries. Oh... I've got custard all over my new dress.'

Poppy giggled. 'That's really *icky*.'

The delicious sound of the child's laughter and that odd word took Catherine straight back to the day she'd met Emma. To that interview for a position that Adam had clearly intended not to give her. He'd been so closed away back then.

Had he had any idea of how unhappy he'd been?

Things couldn't be more different now. Her son was not only happy again, he was happier than he'd ever been. And Emma looked better than she ever had. It had been such a shock to learn she'd been so sick but she'd just had her twelve-month check a couple of weeks ago and the news had been brilliant. Her doctor had told her she had beaten that dreadful disease and he didn't even want to see her again for at least two years.

No wonder Adam was fair glowing with happiness now. She was loving the grin on Adam's face as he listened to Ian's incredulous query.

'Is it really true that Jemima's pregnant? You're going to have *three* donkeys?'

Adam smiled at Emma as he responded. 'The more the merrier.'

Catherine remembered that smile later as she shooed everyone out of the kitchen to deal with the final clearing up. She put some turkey scraps into the dog bowls, wiped the last crumbs of plum pudding from the table and bent to pick up a scrap of paper left over from the crackers that had been pulled.

Had there been something significant in that shared look and smile? Maybe they were waiting for her to join them before making an announcement? Ducking her head beneath a paper chain that was drooping lower than the others and trying not to get her hopes up, Catherine headed for the door.

In the hallway, she had to smile at the wreath of mistletoe crowning the grandfather clock and the big tartan bows on the banister rails. She could hear a guitar being strummed but obviously not by Emma. The enthusiastic but inexpert performance had to be from Ollie, who would probably be taking his treasured Christmas gift to bed with him. Sure enough, as Catherine entered the living room she saw her grandson sitting at Emma's feet as she showed him where to put his fingers to make a chord.

Adam was right beside her on the couch, with his arm around his beloved wife. Poppy was tucked under his other arm and she was holding her favourite gift as well—fluffy drumsticks that she intended to learn to twirl so that one day she could join a real pipe band. The kind her daddy was playing in once again. The dogs weren't far away either as they lay on the rug in front of the fire.

The other sofa and chairs were taken up with the rest of her family and the special friends who'd been invited to celebrate with them. With the backdrop of the enormous Christmas tree and the screwed-up wrapping paper that Holly seemed to think was her special gift, it all added up to being the picture of a perfect Christmas.

How could life get any better than this?

And then Adam spoke and Catherine realised that life could get even better.

'We have something to tell you all,' he said. 'This summer we're going to have a baby.'

'I *know*,' Poppy squeaked. 'Jemima's baby.'

Adam and Emma exchanged a look that brought a lump to Catherine's throat. Had two people ever been so much in love?

'No, pet.' Adam smiled. 'A real baby. Emma's going to be a mummy.'

The shriek of excitement from Marion and Sharon faded as they all noticed Oliver's frown.

'Emma's already a mummy,' he growled. 'She's *our* mummy.'

Emma leaned down to kiss the small boy. 'I am,' she

MILLS & BOON®

Sparkling Christmas sensations!

This fantastic Christmas collection is fit to burst with billionaire businessmen, Regency rakes, festive families and smouldering encounters.

Set your pulse racing with this festive bundle of 24 stories, plus get a fantastic 40% OFF!

Visit the Mills & Boon website today to take advantage of this spectacular offer!

www.millsandboon.co.uk/Xmasbundle

MILLS & BOON®

Want to get more from Mills & Boon?

Here's what's available to you if you join the exclusive **Mills & Boon eBook Club** today:

✦ *Convenience – choose your books each month*
✦ *Exclusive – receive your books a month before anywhere else*
✦ *Flexibility – change your subscription at any time*
✦ *Variety – gain access to eBook-only series*
✦ *Value – subscriptions from just £1.99 a month*

So visit **www.millsandboon.co.uk/esubs** today to be a part of this exclusive eBook Club!